"Peace?" Luc almost spat the word out. "I've had precious little peace since your brother absconded with one million euros and then his temptress of a sister turns up to play sidekick. I warn you now that you will get burned if you think you can play with me and get away with it."

Before Nessa could even think of uttering another word, Luc had pulled her right into him, so that her body was welded to his. All she could feel was whipcord strength and heat.

And then his mouth covered hers, and words were the last thing on Nessa's mind as heat fused with white light to create a scorching trail of fire.

Shock rendered her helpless to Luc's savage sensuality and her own immediately rampant response.

Luc's arm went around her back, arching her into him even more, and ~~his~~
over hers. But this w
it left any other kisse
far distant universe.
unmoved. This was

It was mastery, pure and simple. And
And punishment.

Irish author **Abby Green** ended a very glamorous career in film and TV—which really consisted of a lot of standing in the rain outside actors' trailers—to pursue her love of romance. After she'd bombarded Harlequin with manuscripts, they kindly accepted one, and an author was born. She lives in Dublin, Ireland, and loves any excuse for distraction. Visit abby-green.com or email abbygreenauthor@gmail.com.

Books by Abby Green

Harlequin Presents

Awakened by Her Desert Captor

Rulers of the Desert

A Diamond for the Sheikh's Mistress
A Christmas Bride for the King

Wedlocked!

Claimed for the De Carrillo Twins

Brides for Billionaires

Married for the Tycoon's Empire

One Night With Consequences

An Heir to Make a Marriage
An Heir Fit for a King

Billionaire Brothers

Fonseca's Fury
The Bride Fonseca Needs

Visit the Author Profile page
at Harlequin.com for more titles.

Abby Green

THE VIRGIN'S DEBT TO PAY

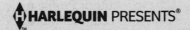

Recycling programs
for this product may
not exist in your area.

ISBN-13: 978-1-335-41933-0

The Virgin's Debt to Pay

First North American publication 2018

Copyright © 2018 by Abby Green

Printed in U.S.A.

THE VIRGIN'S DEBT TO PAY

I'd like to dedicate this story to my go-to Equestrian Experts, Peter Commane and Nemone Routh. Any inaccuracies are all my own fault! And I'd like to thank Heidi Rice, who gave me the moment of inspiration I needed while walking down Pall Mall in London. x

CHAPTER ONE

NESSA O'SULLIVAN HAD never considered herself capable of petty crime, and yet here she was, just outside a private property, under the cover of moonlight, about to break and enter to steal something that didn't belong to her.

She grimaced. Well, to be accurate, she wasn't really going to be breaking and entering, because she had her brother's keys to his office in the Barbier stud farm offices. *Luc Barbier.* Just thinking of the owner of this stud and racing stables made a shiver of apprehension run through Nessa's slim frame. She was crouched under an overhanging branch, on the edge of a pristine lawn in front of the main reception buildings. She'd left her battered Mini Cooper a short distance away from the gates and climbed over a low wall.

Nessa's own family home was not far away, and so she knew the land surrounding this stud farm very well. She'd played here as a child when it was under different ownership.

But any sense of familiarity fled when an owl hooted nearby, and she jumped, her heart slamming against her breastbone. She forced herself to suck in deep breaths to calm her nerves, and cursed her hot-headed older brother again for fleeing like he had. But then, could she really blame Paddy Junior for not standing up to Luc Barbier—the intimidating French *enfant terrible* of the thoroughbred racing world, about whom more was unknown than known?

His darkly forbidding good looks had rumours abounding…that he had been orphaned by gypsies, and that he'd lived on the streets, before becoming something of a legend in the racing world for his ability to train the most difficult of horses.

He'd progressed in a very short space of time to owning his own racing stables outside Paris, and now he owned this extensive stud farm in Ireland attached to another racing stables, where his impressive number of successful racehorses were trained by the best in the world, all under his eagle-eyed supervision.

People said his ability was some kind of sorcery, handed down by his mysterious ancestors.

Other rumours had it that he was simply a common criminal who had grown up on the wrong side of the tracks, and had managed to climb out of the gutter to where he was now by using a fluke talent and ruthless ingenuity to get ahead.

The mystery of his origins only added to the feverish speculation surrounding him, because along with his racing concerns, he had invested in myriad other industries, tripling his fortune in a short space of time and securing his position as one of the world's wealthiest entrepreneurs. But racing and training remained his main concerns.

Paddy Jnr had talked about the man in hushed and awed tones for the last couple of years, since Barbier had employed Nessa's brother as Junior Stud Manager.

Nessa had seen him herself, once or twice, from a distance at the exclusive Irish horse sales—where there was a regular attendance of the most important names in racing from all over the world. Sheikhs and royalty and the seriously wealthy.

He'd stood out, head and shoulders above everyone around him. Inky black hair, thick and wild, touching his collar. A dark-skinned, hard-boned face and a stern expression, his eyes hidden by dark glasses. Thickly muscled arms were folded over his broad chest, and his head had followed the horses as they'd been paraded for the prospective buyers. He'd more resembled the taciturn security guards surrounding some of the sheikhs, or a mysterious movie star, than an owner.

He'd had no obvious security around him, but even now Nessa could recall the faint air of menace keeping people away. He would be well capable of protecting himself.

The only reason she was even here tonight, indulging in this hare-brained exercise for her brother, was because he'd assured her that Luc Barbier was currently in France. She had no desire to come face to face with the man himself, because on those occasions when she had glimpsed him from a distance she'd felt a very disconcerting sensation in her belly—a kind of awareness that was totally alien to her, and very inappropriate to feel towards a complete stranger.

She took another deep breath and moved forward from under the tree, across the lawn to the buildings. A dog barked and Nessa halted, holding her breath. It stopped, and she continued moving forward. She reached the main building and went under the archway that led into a courtyard, around which the administrative offices were laid out.

She followed Paddy's directions and found the main office, and used the bigger key to unlock the door. Her heart was thumping but the door opened without a sound. There was no alarm. Nessa was too relieved to wonder why that might be.

It was dark inside, but she could just about make out the stairs. She climbed them to the upper floor, using the torch app on her phone and breathed a sigh of relief when she found his office. She opened the door with the other key, stepping inside as quietly as she could, before shutting it again. She leant against it for a second, her heart thumping. Sweat trickled down her back.

When she felt slightly calmer she moved further into the office, using her phone to guide her to the desk Paddy had said was his. He'd told her that his laptop should be in the top drawer, but she pulled it open to find it empty. She opened the others but they were empty too. Feeling slightly panicky, she tried the other desks but there was no sign of the laptop. Paddy's frantic words reverberated in her head: *'That laptop is the only chance I have to prove my innocence, if I can just trace the emails back to the hacker...'*

Nessa stood in the centre of the office biting her lip, feeling frantic now herself.

There was no hint of warning or sound to indicate she wasn't alone, so when an internal door in the office opened and light suddenly flooded the room, Nessa only had time to whirl around and blink in shock at the massive figure filling the doorway.

It registered faintly in her head that the man filling the doorway was Luc Barbier. And that she was right to have been wary of coming face to face with him. He was simply the most astonishingly gorgeous and intimidating man she'd ever seen up close, and that was saying something when her brother-in-law was Sheikh Nadim Al-Saqr of Merkazad, as alpha male and masculine as they came.

Luc Barbier was dressed all in black, jeans and a long-sleeved top, which only seemed to enhance his brooding energy. His eyes were deep-set and so dark they looked like fathomless pools. Totally unreadable.

He held up a slim silver laptop and Nessa looked at it stupidly.

'I take it this is what you came here for?'

His voice was low and gravelly and sexily accented, and that finally sent reality slamming back into Nessa like a shot of adrenalin to her heart. She did the only thing she could do—she pivoted on her feet and ran back to the door she'd just come through and pulled it open, only to find a huge burly security guard standing on the other side with a sour expression on his face.

The voice came from behind her again, this time with an unmistakable thread of steel. 'Close the door. You're not going anywhere.'

When she didn't move, the security guard reached past her to pull the door closed, effectively shutting her in with Luc Barbier. Who patently wasn't in France.

With the utmost reluctance she turned around to face him, very aware of the fact that she was wearing black tracksuit bottoms and a close-fitting black fleece with her hair tucked up under a dark baseball cap. She must look as guilty as sin.

Luc Barbier had closed the other door. The laptop was on a desk near him and he was just standing there, arms folded across his chest, legs spread wide as if to be ready for when she bolted again.

He asked, 'So, who are you?'

Nessa's heart thwacked hard. She kept her mouth firmly closed and her gaze somewhere around his impeccably shod feet, hoping the cap would hide her face.

He sighed audibly. 'We can do this the hard way, or the harder way. I can have the police here within ten minutes and you can tell them who you are and why you're trespassing on my property...but we both know it's to get this, don't we?' He tapped the laptop with long fingers where it sat on the desk. 'You're obviously working for Paddy O'Sullivan.'

Nessa barely heard the last phrase. Totally ridiculously, all she could seem to focus on were his beautiful hands. Big and masculine but graceful. Capable hands. *Sexy hands*. The quiver in her belly became something far more disturbing.

Silence lengthened between them again and suddenly Barbier issued a low, violent-sounding curse in French and picked up the laptop, moving towards the door. He was almost there before Nessa realised that involving the Irish Gardaí would be even more of a disaster. The fact that Barbier hadn't called them yet left a sliver of hope that something of this situation could be salvaged.

'Wait!' Her voice sounded very high in the silence.

He stopped at the door, his back to her. It was almost as intimidating as his front. He slowly turned around. 'What did you say?'

Nessa tried to calm her thundering heart. She was afraid to look up too much, using the lip of her cap to keep herself hidden as much as possible.

'I said wait. Please.' She winced. As if a nicety like *please* would go over well in this situation.

There was more silence and then an incredulous-sounding, 'You're a *girl*?'

That struck Nessa somewhere very vulnerable. She knew she was dressed head to toe in black and wore a hat, but was she really so androgynous? She was well aware of her lack of feminine wiles, having spent much of her life knee deep in muck and wellies. She hitched up her chin and glared at him now, too angry to remember to try and stay hidden. 'I'm twenty-four, hardly a girl.'

He looked sceptical. 'Crawling through undergrowth to trespass on private property is hardly the activity of a grown woman.'

The thought of the kind of women a man like this would know—a world away from Nessa—made her skin prickle with self-consciousness and her vulnerability turned into defensiveness. 'You're meant to be in France.'

Luc Barbier was shocked. And he was not a man who was easily shocked. But this slip of a girl—*woman?*—was talking back to him as if she hadn't just flagrantly invaded his private property with clearly criminal intentions.

'I was in France, and now I'm not.'

He allowed his gaze to inspect her more closely, and as he did he felt something infuse his blood... *interest*. Because he could see it now. Yes, she was a woman. Albeit slim and petite to the point of boyishness. But he could see her breasts, small and perfectly formed, pushing against the form-fitting fleece of her black top.

He could make out a jaw too delicate to be a man's, and wondered how he hadn't noticed it before. He also saw a very soft lower lip, which was currently caught between white teeth. He felt a very unwelcome stirring of desire and a need to see more.

'Take off your cap,' he heard himself demand before he'd even registered the impulse.

The small chin came up and that soft lip was freed from white teeth. He saw the tension in her. There was a taut moment when he wasn't sure what she would do. Then, as if realising she had no choice, she raised a small hand and pulled the cap from her head.

For a moment Luc could only stare stupidly as a coil of long, dark red hair fell over her shoulder from where it had been stuffed under the cap.

And then he took in the rest of her face and felt even more foolish. He'd seen countless beautiful women, some of whom were considered to be the most beautiful in the world, but right now they were all an indistinct blur in his memory.

She was stunning. High cheekbones. Flawless creamy pale skin. A straight nose. Huge hazel eyes— flashing green and gold, with long dark lashes. And that mouth, lush and wide.

His body hardened, and the shock of such a reaction to this whippet of a girl made Luc reject the rogue reaction. He did not react to women unless it was on his terms. He was reacting because she was unexpected.

His voice was harsh. 'Now, tell me who you are, or I call the police.'

Nessa burned inwardly from the thorough once-over Barbier had just given her. She felt very exposed without her cap. Exposed to the full impact of him up close. And she couldn't look away. It was as if she were mesmerised by the sun. He was simply... beautiful, in a very raw, masculine way, all hard angles and sharp lines. But his mouth was provocatively sensual—the only softness in that face. It was distracting.

'I'm waiting.'

Nessa flushed, caught out. She diverted her gaze, focusing on a picture of a famous racehorse on the wall behind him. She knew she really didn't have a choice but to give him the information. The alternative was to give it to the Gardaí and, coming from such a small, close-knit community, she knew that word would go around within minutes as to what she had been doing. There was no such thing as privacy or anonymity here.

'My name is Nessa...' She hesitated and then said in a rush, 'O'Sullivan.' She snuck a glance back at Barbier and saw that he was frowning.

'O'Sullivan? You're related to Paddy?'

Nessa nodded miserably at what a disaster this evening's escapade had become. 'I'm his younger sister.'

Barbier took a moment to digest this and then he said, with a curl to his lip, 'He's sending his baby sister to do his dirty work?'

Nessa instantly rose to her brother's defence. 'Paddy is innocent!'

Luc Barbier looked unimpressed by her impassioned outburst. 'He's made a bad situation worse by disappearing, and the facts haven't changed: he facilitated the purchase of a horse from Gio Corretti's Sicilian stud. We received the horse a week ago and the one million euros duly left my account but never reached Corretti's. It's clear that your brother diverted the funds into his own pocket.'

Nessa blanched at the massive amount of money, but she forced herself to stay strong, for Paddy. 'He didn't divert funds. It wasn't his fault. He was hacked   they somehow impersonated the stud manager in Sicily and Paddy sent the money through fully believing it was going to the right place.'

The lines in Barbier's face were as hard as granite. 'If that is the case then why isn't he here to defend himself?'

Nessa refused to let herself crumble in the face of this man's seriously intimidating stance. 'You told him he would be prosecuted and liable for the full amount. He felt as if he had no choice.'

Paddy's frantic voice came back into her head.

'Ness, you don't know what this guy is capable of. He fired one of the grooms on the spot the other day. There's no such thing as innocent till proven guilty in

Barbier's world. He'll chew me up and spit me out! I'll never work in the industry again...'

Barbier's mouth thinned. 'The fact that he fled after that phone conversation only makes him look even guiltier.'

More words of defence sprang to Nessa's lips but she swallowed them back. Trying to explain to this man that her brother had been entangled with the law when he'd gone through a rebellious teenage phase was hardly likely to make him sound less guilty. Paddy had worked long and hard to turn over a new leaf, but he'd been told that if he was ever caught breaking the law again he'd serve time and have a criminal record. *That* was why he'd panicked and run.

Luc Barbier regarded the woman in front of him. The fact that he was still indulging in any kind of dialogue with her was outrageous. And yet her vehemence and clear desire to protect her brother at all costs—even at her own expense—intrigued him. In his experience loyalty was a myth. Everyone was out for their own gain.

Something occurred to him then and he cursed himself for not suspecting it sooner. He'd been too distracted by a fall of thick red hair and a slender frame. It was galling.

'Maybe you're in on it? And you were trying to retrieve the laptop to ensure that any evidence was taken care of?'

Nessa's limbs turned to jelly. 'Of course I'm not

in on anything. I just came here because Paddy—'
She stopped herself, not wanting to incriminate him
further.

'Because Paddy…what?' Barbier asked. 'Was too
much of a coward? Or because he's no longer in the
country?'

Nessa bit her lip. Paddy had fled to America, to
hide out with her twin brother, Eoin. She'd entreated
him to come back, tried to assure him that his boss
couldn't be such an ogre. Paddy's words floated back.

*'No one messes with Barbier. I wouldn't be sur-
prised if he's got criminal links…'*

For a moment Nessa had a sickening sensation.
What if Barbier really *was* linked to—? She quickly
shut that thought down, telling herself she was being
melodramatic. But then a sliver of doubt entered her
mind—what if Paddy *was* guilty?

As soon as that registered she lambasted herself,
aghast that she could have thought it for a second.
This man was making her doubt herself, and her
brother, who she knew would never do something
so wrong, no matter what his trangressions had been
in the past.

Nessa's jaw was tight. 'Look. Paddy is innocent. I
agree with you that he shouldn't have run, but he has.'
She hesitated for a second, and then mentally apolo-
gised to her brother before saying, 'He has a habit of
running away when difficult things happen—he ran
away for a week after our mother's funeral.'

Barbier looked utterly remote and then he said,

'I've heard the Irish have a gift for talking their way out of situations, but it won't work with me, Miss O'Sullivan.'

Anger spiked again. 'I'm not trying to get out of anything.' She forced herself to calm down. 'I was just trying to help by retrieving his laptop. He said that he could prove his innocence with it.'

Barbier picked up the slim silver laptop and held it up. 'We've looked at the laptop extensively and there is no evidence to support your brother's innocence. You've done your brother no favours. He now looks even guiltier and you've possibly implicated yourself.'

Luc watched as colour washed in and out of the woman's expressive face. That in itself was intriguing, when so many people he encountered kept their masks firmly in place. He couldn't recall the last time he'd felt free enough, if ever, to allow his real emotions to be seen.

Still, he wouldn't believe this award-worthy display of innocence. He'd be a fool if he did and her brother had already taken him for a fool.

Nessa sensed any sliver of hope dwindling. Barbier was about as immovable as a rock. He put the laptop down and folded his arms again, settling his hips back against the desk behind him, legs stretched out, for all the world as if they were having a civil chat. There was nothing civil about this man. Danger oozed from every pore: Nessa just wasn't sure what *kind* of danger. She felt no risk to her personal safety, in spite of Paddy's lurid claims or the security man outside the door. It was a much more personal danger, to the place that throbbed with awareness deep inside her. An awareness that had been dormant all her life, until now.

Barbier's tone was mocking. 'So you really expect me to believe that you're here purely out of love for your poor innocent brother?'

Fiercely she said, 'I would do anything for my family.'

'Why?'

Barbier's simple question took her by surprise and Nessa blinked. She hadn't even questioned Paddy when he'd called for help. She'd immediately felt every protective instinct kick into place even though she was younger than him.

Their family was a unit who had come through tough times and become stronger in the process.

Their older sister Iseult had kept them all in one piece—pretty much—after the tragic death of their mother, while their father had descended into the mire of alcoholism. She had shielded Nessa and her two brothers from their father's worst excesses, and had slowly helped him to recovery even as their stud farm and stables had fallen apart around them.

But Iseult wasn't here now. She had a much deserved happy life far away from here. It was up to Nessa to shoulder this burden for the sake of her brother, and her family.

She looked at Barbier. 'I would do anything because we love each other and we protect each other.'

Barbier was silent for a long moment. Then he said, 'So now you're admitting that you'd go so far as to collude in a crime.'

Nessa shivered under the thin covering of her fleece. She felt very alone at that moment. She knew she could contact Sheikh Nadim of Merkazad, Iseult's husband and one of the richest men in the world. He could sort this whole thing out within hours, if he knew. But she and Paddy had agreed they wouldn't involve Iseult or Nadim. They were expecting a baby in a few weeks and did not need to be drawn into this mess.

She squared her shoulders and stared at Luc Barbier, hating his cool nonchalance. 'Don't you understand the concept of family and doing anything for them? Wouldn't you do that for your own family?'

Barbier suddenly looked stony. 'I have no family, so, no, I'm not familiar with the concept.'

A pang of emotion made Nessa's chest tighten. No family. What on earth did that mean? She couldn't fathom the lack of a family. That sense of protection.

Then he said, 'If your family are so close then I will go to whoever *is* capable of returning either your brother or my money.'

Panic eclipsed Nessa's spurt of emotion. 'This just involves me and Paddy.'

Barbier raised a brow. 'I will involve whoever and

whatever it takes to get my money back and ensure no adverse press results from this.'

Nessa's hands clenched to fists at her sides as she tried to contain her temper and appeal to any sense of decency he might have. 'Look, not that it's any business of yours, but my sister is going to have a baby very soon. My father is helping her and her husband and they don't have anything to do with this. I'm taking responsibility for my brother.'

I'm taking responsibility for my brother.

There had been a tight ball of emotion in Luc's chest ever since she'd asked if he understood the concept of family. Of course he didn't. How could he when his Algerian father had disappeared before he was born, and his feckless, unstable mother had died of a drugs overdose when he was just sixteen?

The closest he'd ever come to family was the old man next door—a man broken by life, and yet who had been the one to show Luc a way out.

Luc forced his mind away from the memories. He was beyond incredulous that this sprite of a girl—*woman*—was insisting on standing up to him. And that she wasn't using her beauty to try and distract him, especially when he couldn't be sure that he'd hidden his reaction to her. He hated to admit it, even to himself, but he felt a twinge of respect.

She was defiant, even in the face of possible prosecution. If she was calling his bluff she was doing it very, very well. He could still have the police here within minutes and she would be hauled off in handcuffs with the full weight of his legal team raining down on her narrow shoulders before she knew what was happening.

But it wasn't as if the police were ever first on Luc's list of people to turn to in this kind of situation. Not because he had more nefarious routes to keeping the law—he knew about the rumours surrounding him, and as much as they amused him, they also disgusted him—but because of his experiences growing up in the gritty outskirts of Paris. Surviving each day had been a test of endurance. The police had never been there when he'd needed them, so to say he didn't trust them was an understatement.

He liked to take care of things his own way. Hence the rumours. Added on top of more rumours. Until he was more myth than man.

He forced his mind back to the task at hand. And the woman. 'Where do we go from here, then, Miss O'Sullivan? If you're prepared to take responsibility for your brother, then perhaps you could be so kind as to write me a cheque for one million euros?'

Nessa blanched. One million euros was more money than she was ever likely to see in her lifetime, unless her career as a jockey took off and people started giving her a chance to ride in big races and build her reputation.

She said, as firmly as she could, 'We don't have that kind of money.'

'Well then,' Barbier said silkily, 'that gets us precisely no further along in this situation. And in fact it gets worse. Thanks to your brother's actions, I will now have to hand over another one million euros to Gio Corretti to ensure that he doesn't ask questions about why he hasn't received the money yet.'

Nessa felt sick. She hadn't considered that. 'Maybe you could talk to him? Explain what happened?'

Barbier laughed but it was curt and unamused. 'I don't need to fuel the gossip mill with stories that I'm now claiming fraud to renege on payments.'

Nessa wanted to sit down. Her legs were wobbly again and she felt light-headed.

'Are you all right?' Barbier's sharp question was like a slap to her face. She sucked in a deep breath. He'd taken a step towards her and suddenly the room felt even smaller. He was massive. And so dark. Possibly the most intimidating person she'd ever met.

She couldn't fight this man. He was too rich, too successful. Too gorgeous. She swallowed. 'I wish I could hand you over your money right now, Mr Barbier, believe me. But I can't. I know my brother is innocent no matter what his actions look like.'

Nessa wracked her brains as to what she could do to appease Barbier so he wouldn't go after Paddy. At least until Paddy had a chance to try and prove his innocence. But what could she offer this man? And then something struck her. 'Look, all I can do is offer my services in his absence. If you have *me*, then can't you accept that I'm willing to do all I can to prove his innocence?'

For a moment, Nessa's words hung in the air and she almost fancied that she might have got through to him. But then he straightened from the desk and the expression on his face darkened. He spat out, 'I should have known that veneer of innocence was too good to be true.'

That unnervingly black gaze raked her up and down, disdain etched all over his face. 'I must admit, I might have felt differently if you'd come via the front door dressed in something a little more enticing, Miss O'Sullivan, but even then I can't say that you'd be my type.'

Nessa struggled to understand—he couldn't possibly mean…but then she registered what she'd said and how it might have sounded. And, she registered that he was looking at her with disgust, not disdain. Her gut curdled as a wave of mortification rushed through her whole body, along with hurt, which made it even worse. She burned with humiliation and fury.

'You know I did not mean *that*.'

He raised an imperious brow. 'What did you mean, Miss O'Sullivan?'

Nessa had started to pace in her agitation and she stopped and faced him. 'Please stop calling me that—my name is Nessa.'

His voice was hard. *'Nessa.'*

The way he said her name impacted her physically, like a punch to her gut. She instantly regretted opening her mouth but *Miss O'Sullivan* was beginning to get under her skin. This man. This…

meeting…was veering so far off course that she wasn't even sure what they were talking about any more, or what was at stake.

She tried to force herself to stay focused, and calm. 'What I meant, Mr Barbier, is that I will do everything in my power to convince you that my brother is innocent.'

CHAPTER TWO

LUC STARED AT Nessa O'Sullivan.

I will do everything in my power to convince you that my brother is innocent.

What kind of an empty suggestion was that? And why had it given him such an illicit thrill to see her act so shocked when he'd called her bluff? She'd blatantly offered herself to him—and then pretended that she hadn't!

He wanted to laugh out loud. As if she were an innocent. There was no innocence in this world. Perhaps only in babies, before they grew up to be twisted and manipulated by their environment.

His conscience smarted to think of how he'd told her she wasn't his type. He couldn't deny the pounding of his blood right now. He told himself it was anger. Adrenalin. Anything but helpless desire.

Luc knew he should have walked away long ago and left her at the mercy of the authorities, no matter what he thought of them. He had enough evidence now to damn her, and her brother. But he knew that wasn't necessarily the best option. Not for *him*.

She was staring at him, as if bracing herself for whatever he was going to say. She was throwing up more questions than answers and it had been a long time since anyone had piqued Luc's interest like this.

What did he have to lose if he contained this himself? It wasn't as if the local law enforcement could do any better than the private security company he'd already hired to investigate the matter and track down Paddy O'Sullivan.

One thing was clear. This woman wasn't going to be walking away from here. He didn't trust her. Not one inch of her petite form. Not after he'd seen how far she was prepared to go. And she wasn't going anywhere until he had his money returned and he knew there was no damage to his reputation. If she was involved in this crime, then keeping her close would surely lead him back to the thief.

He folded his arms and saw the way her body tensed, as if to steel herself. In that moment she looked both defiant and vulnerable, and it caught at Luc somewhere he wasn't usually affected. More acting. It had to be. He would not allow her to make a fool of him.

'You say you want to convince me your brother is innocent?'

Nessa still felt sick to think that Barbier had taken her words to mean that she was offering herself up, like some kind of— She forced the thought out of her head. Of course this man would never look at someone like her in that way, but she didn't need to be humiliated.

She tipped up her chin. 'Yes.'

He was looking at her with unnerving intensity. She really couldn't read him at all. Her mouth felt dry and instinctively she licked her lips. His gaze dropped to them for a second and her insides flipped. She ignored it, telling herself her reaction to him was due to the heightened situation.

His eyes met hers again. 'Very well, then. You're not leaving my sight until your brother accounts for his actions and my money is returned.'

Nessa opened her mouth but nothing came out for a moment. Then she said, 'What do you mean, not leaving your sight?'

'Exactly that. You've offered your services in place of your brother, so until he or my money returns you're mine, Nessa O'Sullivan, and you will do exactly as I tell you.'

Nessa struggled to comprehend his words. 'So you're going to hold me as some kind of…collateral? As a prisoner?'

He smiled but it was mirthless. 'Oh, you're quite free to walk out this door, but you won't make it to your car before the police catch up with you. If you want me to believe that you have nothing to do with this, *and* that your brother is innocent, then you will stay here and do your utmost to make yourself useful.'

'How do you know about my car?' Nessa asked, distracted for a moment and not liking the way panic had her insides in a vice grip.

'You were tracked as soon as you parked that heap of junk outside my perimeter wall.'

Fresh humiliation washed over Nessa to think of her stealthy progress being watched in some security room. 'I didn't hear any alarms.'

He dismissed that with a curl of his lip. 'Security here is silent and state of the art. Flashing lights and sirens would unsettle the horses.'

Of course it would. Hadn't Nadim insisted on installing a similarly high-tech system on their own farm? Nessa searched in vain for some way to avoid being forced to spend an unknown amount of time under this man's punitive command, even though she'd all but asked for it. 'I'm a jockey and I work at our family farm—I can't just walk away from that.'

Barbier's black gaze flicked dismissively over her body again before meeting her eyes. 'A jockey? Then how have I never heard of you?'

Nessa flushed. 'I haven't run many races. Yet.' In recent years she'd gone to university and got a degree, so that had taken her out of the circuit for some time. Not that she was about to explain herself to Barbier.

He made a scathing sound. 'I'm sure. Being a jockey is gritty, hard work. You look as if a puff of wind would knock you over. Somehow I can't really see you rousing at dawn and putting in a long day of the back-breaking training and work that most jockeys endure. Your pretty hands would get far too dirty.'

Nessa bristled and instinctively hid her hands behind her back, conscious of how *un*pretty they were, but not wanting to show Barbier, even in her own defence. She still felt raw after his stinging remark, *I can't say that you'd be my type.*

The unfairness of his attack left her a little speechless. Her family had all worked hard at their farm for as long as she could remember, getting up at the crack of dawn every day of the week and in all kinds of weather. Her family had certainly never lived a gilded life of leisure. Not even when Nadim had bought them out and pumped money into their ailing business.

'Who do you ride for, then?'

She forced down the surge in emotion and answered as coolly as she could, 'My family stables, O'Sullivans. I'm well used to doing my share of the work, believe it or not, and I've been training to be a jockey since I was a teenager. Just because I'm a woman—'

He held up a hand stopping her. 'I have no issue with female jockeys. What I do have an issue with are people who get a free pass on their family connections.'

If Nessa had bristled before, now she was positively apoplectic. She'd had to work twice as hard to prove herself to her own family, if not even more.

But she was aware that to really prove herself she'd have to get work with another trainer. It was a sensitive point for her.

'I can assure you,' she said in a low voice full of emotion, 'that my being a jockey is not a vanity project. Far from it.'

She might have laughed if she were able to. Vanity—what was that? She couldn't remember the last time she'd worn make-up.

Barbier looked unimpressed. 'Well, I'm sure the family farm will cope without you.'

Nessa realised that she was damned if she walked out the door and and damned if she didn't. But there was only one way of containing the situation and making sure that the rest of her family weren't dragged into it, and that was doing as Barbier said. She wished she could rewind the clock and be safe at home in bed…but even as she imagined that scenario something inside her rejected it. Rejected the possibility of never having had the opportunity to see this man up close. The shock of that revelation made her stop breathing for a second, its significance terrifying to contemplate.

But the fact was that Nessa's blood was throbbing through her veins in a way she'd never experienced before. Not even after an exhilarating win on a horse.

Shame bloomed deep inside her. How could she betray her own brother, her family, like this? By finding this man so…compelling? Telling herself that stress was making her crazy, she asked, 'What will I be doing here?' She tried to quash lurid images of herself, locked in a tower being fed only bread and water.

Barbier's eyes flicked up and down over her body as if gauging what she might be capable of. Nessa bristled all over, again.

'Oh, don't worry, we'll find something to keep you occupied, and of course any work you do will be in lieu of payment. Until your brother resurfaces, his debt is now yours.'

Barbier straightened up to his full intimidating height and Nessa's pulse jumped.

'I will have Armand escort you back to your home to retrieve what you need. You can give me your car keys.'

This was really happening. And there was nothing she could do about it. Nessa reluctantly reached into her pocket for her keys and took the car key off the main ring, all fingers and thumbs. Eventually she got it free, skin prickling under the laser-eyed scrutiny of Barbier.

She handed it over, a little devil inside her prompting her to say, 'It's a vintage Mini. I doubt you'll fit.' Even the thought of this man coiling his six-foot-plus frame into her tiny battered car was failing to spark any humour in the surreal moment. She really hadn't expected the night to turn out like this… and yet she could see now that she'd been supremely naive to assume it would be so easy to infiltrate the Barbier stud.

He took the key. 'It won't be me retrieving your car.'

Of course. It would be a minion, despatched to take care of the belongings of the woman who was now effectively under house arrest for the foreseeable future.

Not usually given to dramatics, Nessa tried to quell her nerves. She was within five kilometres of her own home, for crying out loud. What was the worst this man could do to her? A small sly voice answered that the worst he could do had nothing to do with punishment for Paddy's sins, and everything to do with how he made her feel in his presence. As if she were on a roller coaster hurtling towards a great swooping dip.

Barbier turned away and opened the office door to reveal the huge burly man still standing outside. They spoke in French so rapid that it was beyond Nessa's basic grasp of the language to try and understand what they were saying.

Barbier turned back to her, switching to English. 'Armand will escort you home to collect your things and bring you back here.'

'Can't I just return in the morning?'

He shook his head, looking even more stern now, and indicated for her to precede him. Mutely, Nessa stepped over the threshold and followed the thickset security man back out the way she'd come. In the courtyard there was a sleek four-by-four car waiting. Armand opened a car door for her.

For a second Nessa hesitated. She saw the entrance to the courtyard and a glimpse of freedom, if she moved fast. From behind her she heard a deep voice. 'Don't even think about it.'

She turned around. Barbier was right behind her and looked even more intimidating in the dark. Taller, more austere. His face was all hard bones and slashing angles. Not even the softness of that provocative mouth visible.

Nessa put her hand on the car door, needing something to hold onto. 'What happens when I come back?'

'You'll be informed when you do.'

Panic made her blurt out, 'What if I refuse?'

She saw the gallic shrug. 'It's up to you but you've made it clear you don't want to involve your family. If you refuse to return I can guarantee that *that* will be the least of your worries. You would be an accessory to a crime.'

Nessa shivered again in the cool, night-time air. She had no choice, and he knew it. Defeated, she turned and stepped up into the vehicle, and the door closed behind her.

The windows were tinted and Nessa was enclosed in blackness as the bodyguard came around the front of the vehicle and got into the driver's seat. Barbier strode away from them towards the main building and she felt suddenly bereft, which was ridiculous when the man was holding her to ransom for her brother. *You put yourself up for that ransom*, a voice reminded her.

As they approached the main gates Nessa reluctantly gave Armand directions to her own home. They passed her lonely-looking car on the side of the road and she sucked in a deep breath, telling herself that if she could endeavour to persuade Paddy to return to prove his innocence, and prevent anyone else from getting involved, then this—hopefully!—brief punishment at the hands of Barbier would be worth it.

Nessa tried to call up her usually positive disposition. Surely if Barbier saw how far she was willing to go to prove her brother's innocence, he'd be forced to reconsider and give Paddy a chance to explain, wouldn't he?

But why was it that that seemed to hold less appeal than the thought of seeing Luc Barbier again? Nessa scowled at herself in the reflection of the tinted window of the car, glad she wasn't under that black-eyed gaze when her face got hot with humiliation.

When Nessa returned a short while later the stud was in darkness and quiet. Armand handed her over to a middle-aged man with a nice face who looked as if he'd just been woken up, and he was not all that welcoming. He introduced himself as Pascal Blanc, Barbier's stud and racing stables manager, his right-hand man, and Paddy's one-time immediate boss.

He said nothing at first, showing her to a small spartan room above the stables. Clearly this was where the most menial staff slept. But still, it was clean and comfortable, when Nessa had almost expected a corner of the stables.

After giving her the basics of the Barbier stud schedule and informing her that, naturally, she would be assigned to mucking out the yard and stables, and to expect a five a.m. wake-up call, he stopped at her door. 'For what it's worth, I would have given Paddy the benefit of the doubt based on what I thought I knew of him. We might have been able to get to the bottom of this whole nasty incident. But he ran, and now there's nothing I can do except hope for his sake and yours that he either returns himself or returns the money. Soon.'

Nessa couldn't say anything.

Pascal's mouth compressed. 'Luc... Mr Barbier... does not take kindly to those who betray him. He comes from a world where the rule of law didn't exist and he doesn't suffer fools, Miss O'Sullivan. If your brother *is* guilty, then Luc won't be gentle with him. Or you.'

Somehow these words coming from this infinitely less intimidating man made everything even bleaker. But all Nessa could find herself doing was asking, 'You've known Mr Barbier for long?'

Pascal nodded. 'Ever since he started to work with Leo Fouret, the first time he came into contact with a horse.'

Nessa was impressed. Leo Fouret was one of the most respected trainers in racing, with hundreds of impressive race wins to his name.

'Luc didn't grow up in a kind world, Miss O'Sullivan. But he is fair. Unfortunately your brother never gave him that chance.'

Luc didn't grow up in a kind world... The words reverberated in Nessa's head for a long time after she'd been left alone in the room. She eventually fell into a fitful sleep and had dreams of riding a horse, trying to go faster and faster—not to get to the finish line but to escape from some terrifying and unnamed danger behind her.

What on earth did she have to laugh about? Luc was distinctly irritated by the faint lyrical sound emanating from his stableyard, which was usually a place of hushed industry in deference to the valuable livestock. It could only be coming from one person, the newest addition to his staff: Nessa O'Sullivan.

Her brother had stolen from him and now she laughed. It sent the very insidious thought into Luc's head that he'd been a total fool. Of course she was in on it with her brother and now she was inside the camp. It made him think of the Trojan Horse and he didn't find it amusing.

He cursed and threw down his pen and stood up from his desk, stalking over to the window that looked down over the stables. He couldn't see her and that irritated him even more when he'd deliberately avoided meeting her since her arrival, not wanting to give her the idea that their extended dialogue the other night would ever be repeated. Now he was distracted. When he couldn't afford to be distracted.

He'd only just managed to convince Gio Corretti that the slight delay in money arriving to his account was due to a banking glitch.

Luc's reputation amongst the exclusive thoroughbred racing fraternity had been on trial since he'd exploded onto the scene with a rogue three-year-old who had raced to glory in four consecutive Group One races.

Success didn't mean respect though. He was an anomaly; he had no lineage to speak of and he'd had the temerity to invest wisely with his winnings and make himself a fortune in the process.

Everyone believed his horses were better bred than he was, and they weren't far wrong. The rumours about his background merely added colour to every other misconception and untruth heaped against his name.

But, as much as he loved ruffling the elite's feathers by making no apology for who he was, he *did* want their respect. He wanted them to respect him for what he had achieved with nothing but an innate talent, hard work and determination.

The last thing he needed was for more rumours to get around, especially one suggesting that Luc Barbier couldn't control his own staff. That he'd been stupid enough to let one million euros disappear from his account.

Even now he still felt the burn of recrimination for

finding Paddy O'Sullivan's open expression and infectious enthusiasm somehow quaint. He should have spotted a thief a mile away. After all, he'd grown up with them.

Luc tensed when he heard the faint sound of laughing again. Adrenalin mixed with something far more ambiguous and hotter flooded his veins. Nessa O'Sullivan was here under sufferance for her brother—and that was all. The sooner she remembered her place and what was at stake, the better.

'Who were you talking to?'

Nessa immediately tensed when she heard the deep voice behind her. She turned around reluctantly, steeling herself to see Barbier for the first time since that night. And she blinked.

The skies were blue and the air was mild but, in that uniquely Irish way, there seemed to be a mist falling from the sky and tiny droplets clung to Barbier's black hair and shoulders, making him look as if he were…sparkling.

His hands were placed on lean hips. Dark worn jeans clung to powerful thighs and long legs. He was wearing a dark polo shirt. The muscles of his biceps pushed against the short sleeves, and the musculature of his impressive chest was visible under the thin material.

He couldn't look more virile or vitally masculine if he tried. Nessa's body hummed in helpless reaction to that very earthy and basic fact.

'Well?'

Nessa was aghast at how she'd just lost it there for a second, hypnotised by his sheer presence.

She swallowed. 'I was just talking to one of the grooms.'

'You do realise you're not here to socialise, don't you, O'Sullivan?'

Tendrils of Nessa's hair escaped the hasty bun she'd piled on her head earlier, and whipped around her face in the breeze. Her skin prickled at her reaction to him and irritation made her voice sharp. 'It's hard to forget when I've been assigned little more than a cell to sleep in and a pre-dawn wake-up call every day.'

She was very conscious of the unsubtle stench of horse manure clinging to her. And of her worn T-shirt tucked into even more worn jeans. Ancient knee-high boots. She couldn't be any less his *type* right now.

A calculating glint turned his eyes to dark pewter. 'You assured me you were accustomed to hard work and you did offer your services in the place of your brother—if this is too much for you…' He put out a hand to encompass the yard around them.

Nessa stiffened at the obvious jibe. He was clearly expecting her to flounce out of here in a fit of pique. And yes, the work was menial but it was nothing she hadn't done since she'd started walking and could hold a broom. That, and riding horses. Not that he'd believe her.

She squared her shoulders and stared him down. 'If you don't mind, the yard has to be cleaned by lunchtime.'

Barbier looked at the heavy platinum watch encircling his wrist, and then back to her. 'You'd better keep going then, and next time don't distract my employees from their own work. Flirting and gossiping won't help your brother out of his predicament or make things any easier for you here.'

Flirting? For a second Nessa's mind was blank with indignation when she thought of the groom she'd been talking to—a man in his sixties. But before she could think of anything to say in her own defence, Barbier had turned his back and was walking away.

In spite of her indignation, Nessa couldn't stop her gaze following his broad back, seeing how it tapered down to those slim hips and a taut behind, lovingly outlined by the soft worn material of his jeans. He disappeared around a corner and Nessa deflated like a balloon. She turned around in disgust at herself for being so easily distracted, and riled.

Feeling thoroughly prickly and with her nerves still jangling, Nessa turned the power-hose machine back on and imagined Barbier's too-beautiful and smug face in every scrap of dirt she blasted into the drains.

'She's totally over-qualified, Luc. She's putting my own staff to shame, doing longer hours. I shouldn't even be saying this but the yard and stables have never been so clean.' Luc's head groom laughed but soon stopped when Luc fixed him with a dark look.

'No, you shouldn't. Maybe you need new staff.'

Simon Corrigan swallowed and changed the subject. 'Can I ask why we're not paying her? It seems—'

'No, you can't.' Luc cut him off, not liking the way his conscience was stinging. He was many things, but no one had ever faulted him on his sense of fairness and equality. But only he and Pascal Blanc knew what was behind Paddy O'Sullivan's sudden disappearance, and he wanted to keep it that way.

Nessa had been working at his stables for a week now. She hadn't turned tail and run or had a tantrum as he'd expected. He could still see her in his mind's eye—standing in the yard the other day, her back as straight as a dancer, face flushed, amber-green eyes bright and alive. That soft lush mouth compressed. Long tendrils of dark red hair clinging to her hot cheeks as she'd obviously struggled to keep her temper in check.

Her T-shirt had been so worn he could make out the shape of her breasts—small, lush swells, high and firm.

He could also remember the feeling that had swept through him when he'd heard her carefree laugh. It hadn't been anger that she might be up to something. It had been something much hotter and ambiguous; a sense of possessiveness that had shocked him. It wasn't something he felt for anything much, except horses or business acquisitions.

'Where is she now?' Luc asked Corrigan abruptly.

'She's helping to bring the stallions in from the paddocks. Do you want me to give her a message?'

Luc shook his head. 'No, I'll do it.'

But when Luc got to the stallions' stables Nessa was nowhere to be seen and all the stallions had been settled for the evening. Feeling a mounting frustration, he went looking for her.

'You are a beautiful boy, aren't you? Yes, you are… and you know it too. Yes, there you go…' The three-year-old colt whinnied softly in appreciation as he took the raw carrot from Nessa's hand and she rubbed his nose.

She knew she shouldn't be here in the racing section of Barbier's stables, where the current thorough-breds resided, but she hadn't been able to resist. She felt at peace for the first time in days, even as her body actually ached with the need to feel a horse underneath her with all that coiled power and strength and speed. But she wouldn't be riding again for a while.

'You were told to stay away from this area.'

And just like that Nessa's short-lived sense of peace vanished and was replaced by an all-too predictable jump in her heart-rate. She turned around to see Barbier standing a few feet away, arms folded. He was wearing a white shirt, and it made his skin look even darker. His hair touched the collar, curling slightly.

'I'm on a break,' she responded defensively, wondering if he was this autocratic with all his employees. But she had to admit that, so far, everyone seemed pretty content to be working here. She'd found out that the employee who'd been fired on the spot had been smoking weed and she'd had to concede that he would have suffered a similar fate on their own stud farm. Barbier had also enrolled the employee on an addiction course. It was disconcerting to realise that perhaps he wasn't as ruthless as she'd like to believe.

Barbier moved now and closed the distance between them before she could take another breath. He snatched the rest of the carrot out of her hand, frowning. 'What are you feeding Tempest?'

'It's just a carrot.' She pulled her hand back into her chest disconcerted by the shock his fleeting touch had given her.

He glared at her, and he was far too close, but Nessa's back was against the stall door and the horse. She was trapped.

'No one is allowed to feed my horses unless they're supervised.'

Her mouth dropped open and then she sputtered, 'It's just a carrot!'

He was grim. 'A carrot that could contain poison or traces of steroids for all I know.'

Nessa went cold. 'You think I would harm your horses?'

His jaw was as hard as granite. 'I'm under enough scrutiny as it is. I don't need the possible accomplice of a thief messing around with my valuable livestock. I don't know what you're capable of. How did you know that this is the horse?'

Nessa struggled to keep up. '*What* horse?'

Now Barbier was impatient. 'The horse I bought from Gio Corretti.'

Nessa swallowed. 'I had no idea, I just came in for a visit. He seemed agitated.'

Barbier's gaze went from her to the horse behind her and she took the opportunity to slide sideways, putting some distance between them. He put out a hand and stroked the side of Tempest's neck, murmuring soft words in French. Nessa's gaze locked onto his big hand stroking the horse, and she had to struggle not to imagine how that hand might feel on her. She'd never in her life imagined a man stroking her—she must be losing her mind.

The horse pushed his head into Barbier's hand and Nessa glanced at Barbier to see his features relax slightly. For a heady moment she imagined that there was no enmity between them and that he might not always look at her as if she'd just committed a crime. She wondered what he'd look like if he smiled and then she glanced away quickly, mortified at herself and afraid he would read her shameful thoughts on her face.

Barbier said, 'He's been agitated since he arrived, not settling in properly.'

Welcoming the diversion from her wayward imagination, Nessa replied, 'He's probably just pining for his mother.'

Barbier looked at her sharply, his hand dropping away. 'How would you know such a thing?'

Nessa flushed and kept avoiding his eye. How could she explain the weird affinity for horses that she shared with her sister and father? She shrugged. 'I just guessed.'

Barbier's voice was harsh. 'Gio Corretti told me and your brother that we might have issues settling the colt because he hadn't been separated from his mother until recently, which is unusual. That's how you know.'

Nessa looked at Barbier and saw the condemnation and distrust in his eyes. How could she defend a gut feeling? She shrugged and looked away. 'If you say so.'

Without realising it, Nessa's hand had instinctively lifted up to touch the horse again, until suddenly Barbier reached out and took it. Nessa jumped at the weird electricity that sparked whenever they got too close. She tried to pull her hand back but his grip was too firm. And warm.

He was holding her palm facing upwards, and asked grimly, 'What is this?'

She looked down and saw what he saw: her very *un*pretty hands, skin roughened from her training as a jockey and blistered from the last few days of hard work. Humiliated at the thought that he'd see this as proof she wasn't used to work, she yanked her hand back and cradled it to her chest again. 'It's nothing.'

She backed away towards the entrance. 'I should go—my break is over.' She turned and forced herself to walk and not run away, not even sure what she was running from. But something about the way he'd just taken her hand and looked so disapproving to see the marks of her labour made her feel incredibly self-conscious and also a little emotional, which was truly bizarre.

Nessa couldn't recall the last time anyone had focused attention on her like that. Her sister had done her best but she wasn't their mother. Their father hadn't been much use while he'd drowned his sorrows.

So they'd had to fend for themselves mostly. She hadn't even realised until that moment how much another's touch could pierce her right to the core. And for it to have been Luc Barbier was inconceivable and very disturbing. She didn't have an emotional connection with that man—the very notion was ridiculous.

Luc watched as Nessa walked quickly out of the stables and around the corner with an easy athletic grace that made him wonder what she'd be like on a horse. *Excellent*, his instincts told him, as much as he'd like to ignore them.

He was still astounded at the apparent ease with which she'd calmed Tempest, who was one of the most volatile horses Luc had ever bought. But also potentially one of the best, if his hunch about the colt's lineage was right. Certainly Gio Corretti had asked for top dollar, so he'd clearly suspected potential greatness too.

Luc turned back to the horse, who pushed his face into Luc's shoulder, nudging. Did Luc really believe Nessa would poison the horse? He held up the innocuous, gnarled carrot and eventually fed it to the horse with a sigh.

The answer came from his gut: no, she wouldn't poison his horse. She'd looked too shocked when he'd said it. But the fact was that, until her brother reappeared or the money did, the jury was out on Nessa O'Sullivan and he had to keep her under close scrutiny. He'd be a fool not to suspect that brother and sister were working in tandem.

Luc told himself it was for this reason, and *not* because her raw hands had twisted something inside his gut, that he was about to move her to where she could be kept under closer scrutiny.

CHAPTER THREE

'I'M MOVING YOU out of the stables and into the house.'

Nessa looked at Luc Barbier where he stood behind his desk. She'd been summoned here a few minutes ago by the head groom, Simon Corrigan, and she'd tried not to let the understated luxury of the grand old Irish country house intimidate her.

This was where Barbier's suite of private offices were based and now she stood on thick sumptuous carpet and was surrounded by dark oak panelling. Books filled floor-to-ceiling shelves. In contrast to the rather conservative decor, there was modern art on the walls that tickled at Nessa's curiosity. And behind Barbier, a massive window where Nessa could see the training gallops in the distance. An amazing view and one that made her yearn to be on a horse.

But she dragged her attention back to what he'd said. 'Excuse me?'

'I said, I'm moving you into the house.' He enunciated the words slowly, which only made his accent more noticeable. Nessa still couldn't get over the raw, untameable energy that emanated from the man, in spite of the luxe surroundings.

She felt a bit dense. 'Why?'

'My housekeeper has lost one of her household assistants and so I told her you would fill in.'

'Household assistant,' Nessa said slowly as it sank in. 'You mean a cleaner?'

Barbier grimaced faintly. 'I think they prefer the term household assistant.'

A faint burn of humiliation washed up through her body. 'This is because I went to see your racehorses.'

Barbier's jaw tightened. 'I'm not so petty.'

Nessa thought of being cooped up indoors cleaning floors and already felt claustrophobic. 'You accused me of potential sabotage.'

Barbier's jaw got even tighter. 'At this point in time I have no idea what you're capable of. You've put yourself in this position in a bid to convince me your brother is innocent. Mrs Owens, my housekeeper, needs someone to help her out—'

'And I'm just the handy house-arrest guest you can move about at will to wherever it suits you,' Nessa interrupted, feeling frustrated and angry.

'You're the one who is here by choice, Nessa. By all means you're free to walk out this door at any time, but if you do I won't hesitate to involve the local police.'

Nessa tipped up her chin, feeling reckless. 'So why don't you do it, then? Just call them!'

Barbier didn't look remotely fazed at her outburst.

'Because,' he said easily, 'I don't believe it serves either of our interests to involve the law at this point. Do you really want to drag your family name into the open and inform everyone of what your brother has done?'

Nessa went cold inside when she thought of the lines of pain already etched into her father's face. Indelible lines that would never fade even in spite of his much better mental state. She thought of Iseult's frantic worry and her husband, Nadim, who would undoubtedly storm in to take over—just weeks before their baby was due.

Nessa looked at the man in front of her and hated him at that moment. Hated the way he was able to hold her to ransom so easily, and then that hatred turned inwards. She only had herself to blame. And Paddy.

She had taken responsibility and she couldn't crumble now.

She forced down an awful feeling of futility and said, 'No, I don't want anyone to know what has happened. If I stay and do as you ask, can you promise that you won't report what Paddy has done?'

Barbier inclined his head slightly. 'Like I said, it serves us both to keep this to ourselves for the time being.'

Nessa wondered why he was so reluctant to let this get out, but then she realised that he would hardly like it to be known that payment for a horse had gone astray. It would put off potential sellers everywhere.

For a fleeting moment Nessa considered threatening to leak this news in return for Barbier's assurance that Paddy wouldn't be prosecuted. But she realised, without even testing him, that Barbier was not a man who could be so easily manipulated.

Apart from which, she didn't have the stomach for blackmail, and there would be no way that Paddy's reputation could remain unsullied. He might never get the chance to prove his innocence, and with the stain of possible theft and corruption on his record he'd never get a job in the industry he loved again. It would ruin him. Not to mention the disappointment of their father and sister...

As if privy to her thoughts, Barbier said, 'You're the only insurance Paddy has at the moment. His only guarantee of any kind of protection. You walk out of here and that's gone, along with any sliver of doubt I may have about his guilt.'

Nessa's heart thumped hard at that. So there *was* a chance that Barbier might believe in Paddy, if she could just convince him to return and explain what had happened. She had to cling onto that.

Not even sure what she wanted to say but wanting to capitalise on any sliver of mercy she could, she started, 'Mr Barbier—'

'It's Luc,' he cut her off. 'I don't stand on ceremony with anyone, not even a suspected thief.'

He didn't trust her as far as he could throw her, yet he would still allow her to call him by his first name. Nessa didn't like how his bad opinion of her affected her. She'd never done a dishonest thing in her life—apart from creeping onto this property on that fateful night.

She told herself that she just didn't like anyone thinking badly of her—and that Barbier's opinion of her wasn't important. But that felt like a lie.

'Fine, I'll work in the house.'

The corner of his mouth tipped up ever so slightly in a mocking smile. 'I like how you give yourself the illusion of having a choice.'

Nessa controlled her facial expression, not wanting to let him know how much he got to her. 'Was that all?'

Now he looked slightly frustrated, as if he'd expected something else from her. After a moment he just said coolly, 'Yes, Mrs Owens will send for you and show you what she needs. You'll move into one of the staff bedrooms here.'

So she was to be completely removed from the realm of the stud farm and racing stables. Her heart contracted at the thought of being away from the horses, but at the same time an illicit fizz started in her body at the realisation that she'd be sleeping under the same roof as Barbier—*Luc*.

She'd never be able to say his name out loud; it felt far too intimate.

And not that she'd even see him, she assured herself. Not that she *wanted* to see him! She'd probably be confined to cleaning bathrooms and vacuuming hallways. Nessa left his office with as much dignity as she could muster.

En route back to her own quarters, she diverted and went to the paddocks where the stallions idly grazed the lush grass.

One of the huge beasts came over and whinnied, pushing his face into Nessa's shoulder. She dutifully pulled out the ubiquitous carrot she always carried and fed it to him, stroking his soft nose and feeling ridiculously at sea.

Being sequestered indoors and kept away from the bucolic expanse and the animals was more of a punishment than mucking out stableyards and stables ever could be. But Nessa couldn't convince herself that Barbier was doing it out of spite. He really didn't seem that petty.

Instead, she couldn't stop thinking about how he'd taken her hand in his and looked at her rough skin so fiercely the other day. She'd felt self-conscious ever since then. She curled her hands inwards now and shoved them back into her pockets, backing away from the horse.

As she walked back to the main buildings she told herself it was ridiculous to imagine for a second that Barbier had moved her away from the stables for any other reason than just because she was bound to serve out her time here however he willed it.

The man couldn't care less about her labour-worn hands, and, anyway, hot soapy water and housework were hardly going to be any less taxing or more gentle! She just had to get on with it and make the best of this situation until they could prove Paddy's innocence.

It took a long time for the heat in Luc's body to die down after Nessa had left his office. He'd had to battle the urge to push his desk aside and take that stubborn chin in his thumb and forefinger, tipping it up so that she presented her lush mouth to his. Silencing her in a way that would be unbelievably satisfying.

It was confounding. And irritating as hell. Especially as she was wearing nothing more provocative than a worn T-shirt, jeans and boots, hair pulled back in a messy ponytail and no make-up. Yet there was something very earthy and sensual about her that made her all woman.

That, and the defiant tilt of her jaw and the look in her eyes, effortlessly enflamed him. He had the same impulse when he was around her that he had with an unbroken horse. A desire to tame it, and make it bend to his will.

He'd never before become so interested in one woman. Women had never enthralled Luc beyond the initial attraction, and it usually waned quickly. He'd be the first to admit his experience of women hadn't been the most rounded. His mother had shown only the briefest moments of motherly love, before her addictions had swallowed her whole.

The girls in his milieu had been as gritty and tough as him, broken by their surroundings and circumstances. And if they weren't broken then they got out and went far away, exactly as he had done.

Sometimes, the women who frequented the social sphere he now inhabited reminded him of the girls and women of his youth. They were hard and gritty too, but hid it under a shiny, expensive sheen.

But Nessa was none of those things, which intrigued him in spite of his best instincts. And she was out of bounds, for many reasons, not least of which was her suspected collusion with her brother.

He knew without arrogance that she was attracted to him. He saw it in her over-bright eyes and pink cheeks, her taut body that quivered slightly in his presence. He felt fairly sure she must know that he was attracted to her—in spite of his words that first night. *I can't say that you'd be my type.* Apparently she was.

Yet she wasn't testing him by using their chemistry to try and leverage any advantage. He didn't think a woman existed who wouldn't. Unless she was playing some game. *That* was far more probable.

He stood at his window now, the view encompassing the gallops in the distance where his thoroughbreds were being exercised, and the stud farm just out of sight on the other side.

He had both sides of the industry here—racing and breeding. It gave him immense satisfaction to see it all laid out before him, except today, for the first time, there was a slight dilution of that satisfaction. As if something had taken the sheen off it.

As if something was reminding him that he hadn't made it yet. Not really.

Luc scowled. He knew he hadn't made it yet, not completely. No matter how many winners he had or sired with his stallions.

He wouldn't have made it until he was respected by his peers, and not looked at with varying degrees of suspicion.

It was the only fulfilment he wanted. He had no desire for the things most normal people wanted—family, security, love. What was love anyway? It was a foreign concept to Luc that came far too close to believing in trust, and such notions as fate and chance.

He couldn't understand Nessa's blind defence of her brother—unless she was getting something out of it too. It was inconceivable she was doing it out of pure affection or loyalty.

All that existed for him were the solid successes he'd manifested out of sweat and dogged ambition. The legacy he would leave behind would tell a different story from the one he'd been handed at birth. His name would endure as a gold standard in racing.

And yet now, for the first time, he had the disquieting suspicion that even if every one of his peers were to look him in the eye with the utmost respect, he'd still feel less than them.

A movement to the far right in the stud stableyard area caught Luc's eye and he welcomed the distraction. He turned his head just in time to catch a flash of dark red hair coiling down a slim back before

Nessa disappeared around a corner. His reaction was instant and intense, making him scowl even harder at his body's lack of control.

His body pulsed with need. He should be pushing this woman further away, leaving it to his staff to keep her in check. But instead he was bringing her closer.

He was experiencing a kind of hunger he'd only felt once before, when he'd had his first taste of the wider world outside the gloomy Parisian suburbs and had made the vow to never end up back there again. He'd taken that hunger, and used it.

This hunger, however, would be crushed. Because it could do nothing to enhance his success, or his life. Resisting her would be a test of his will to not demean himself.

'Here—last job of the day, love, go up and do the boss's private suite. He's due back from Paris later this evening and I never had a chance to get around to it, what with the preparations for the party this weekend.'

Nessa took the basket containing cleaning products from Mrs Owens and hated that her skin got hot just at the mention of *the boss* and that he was returning soon. He'd been at his Paris stables for the past three days, which hadn't felt as much of a respite as Nessa had thought it would.

Angry with herself for still being so aware of him when he wasn't even here, she focused on feeling relieved that the day was nearly over. There was something particularly soul-sucking about doing housework all day, every day, and as Nessa had polished the silver earlier she'd revised her opinion that Luc Barbier wasn't petty.

They'd also been busy preparing for a huge party that was being thrown at the house that weekend, to launch the most prestigious racing event in the Irish season.

Just as the homely housekeeper was turning away she stopped and said, 'I've left fresh bedlinen in his room, so just strip the bed and remake it. Once you're done with that you're off for the evening.'

Nessa went upstairs to the second floor of the villa-style country house, still marvelling at the opulence. It was about two hundred years old. All the bedroom suites were on the second floor. The first floor was taken up with Barbier's—*Luc's*—office and a gym. There was also a vast media room with a private cinema and informal meetings rooms.

The ground floor held the grand ballroom—prepared for the party now—with French doors opening out onto exquisite manicured gardens. It also had the main, and less formal, dining rooms and reception rooms.

The basement was where the vast kitchen and staff quarters were laid out. All in all a very grand affair. It certainly put Nessa's family farmhouse to shame, even though it too had been refurbished to a high standard since Iseult had married Nadim. It was a far more modestly sized house, though.

Nessa reached the second floor, and walked to the end of the corridor past all the guest rooms to where Luc's rooms were based. He had one entire wing, and she found she was holding her breath slightly as she opened the door.

His scent hit her instantly. Woody and musky. It curled through her nose and deep into the pit of her belly. Cursing herself for her reaction, she strode into the main reception room, dumping the basket of cleaning supplies and resolutely opening the sash windows to let some air in. She told herself the room was musty, not musky and provocative.

Still, she couldn't help but look around. The room was huge and open plan, with soft grey furnishings in muted tones. The same stunning modern art that she'd seen in his office was dotted around the walls, along with sculptures, huge coffee-table books on photography, art, and movies. More books than she'd ever seen in her life, ranging from thrillers to the classics.

The decor and objects reflected a far more cerebral man than Nessa would have guessed existed under Barbier's brooding, sexy exterior.

She had to force herself to remember why she was here and not give into the impulse to pluck out a book from the shelves and curl up on one of the sumptuous couches to read. She realised that she was more weary than she'd realised—the stress of the situation and hard work, mixed with nights of fitful sleep, wasn't a good combination. But she wasn't a wilting lily, and normally worked harder than most, so it annoyed her to find herself feeling tired now.

She scooped up the cleaning supplies and set to work dusting and cleaning. Eventually, as if she'd been putting it off, she went into the bedroom area. She opened the doors and the first thing that hit her eyeline was the bed. It was massive, dominating the room. Much like the man.

It was a modern bed with a dark grey headboard that reminded her ridiculously of his eyes and how they could turn dark silver. A detail she shouldn't even be aware of.

Apart from the bed there were some built-in wardrobes, a sleek chest of drawers and bedside tables. What was striking was the absence of anything of particularly personal value. No photos. No *stuff.* Just some clothes draped on one of the chairs and the rumpled bedsheets, which she avoided looking at.

Then she spied two more doors that revealed a walk-in closet and a luxurious bathroom complete with wetroom shower and a tub that looked big enough to take a football team.

Nessa set about cleaning the bathroom, trying not to breathe in his scent, which was everywhere. She picked up a bottle of cologne and guiltily sniffed it before putting it down again hastily.

Disgusted with herself, she finished cleaning and

went back into the bedroom, pulling off the crumpled sheets and trying not to imagine that they were still warm from his body. *Would he sleep naked? He seems like the kind of man who would...*

Nessa stopped dead for a moment, shocked at the vivid turn of her imagination, and at the way she suddenly hungered to know what he would look like—imagining the sexy naked sprawl of that big bronzed body all too easily, and knowing her imagination probably fell far short of reality. Her pulse became slow and hot.

She had to face the unpalatable fact that Luc Barbier had succeeded where no other man had. He'd awoken her hormones from their dormant state. *Their virginal state.* And it was beyond humiliating that the first man she should feel lust for was the last man who would ever look at her like that.

She'd often wondered why she'd never felt particularly roused by other boys' kisses at university, and her lack of response had earned her a reputation of being standoffish. She'd closed inwards after that, choosing to avoid exposing herself and risk being mocked.

Nessa made the bed as clinically as she could, ignoring the faint dent near the centre that indicated where he slept. When she was done she made one more sweep of the rooms to make sure she hadn't missed anything and collected all the cleaning materials. She stepped inside the bedroom one last time to run her eye over the now-pristine bed and was about to step back out and shut the door when something caught her eye outside.

She went over to the window, putting the basket down for a moment. The view took her breath away; the sun was setting over the gallops, bathing everything in a lush golden light. There were no horses being exercised now, but Nessa could remember how it felt to harness a thoroughbred's power as it surged powerfully beneath her. There was a wide window seat and Nessa sat down, curling her legs underneath her, enjoying the view for an illicit moment.

Nessa suspected that she knew exactly why she had avoided physical intimacy until now. Their mother's death had profoundly affected everyone in her family: Iseult had grown up overnight to become their mother and much more, and the boys had gone off the rails in their own ways but had always turned to each other. Even though Nessa was a twin to Eoin, they'd never had that bond people spoke of.

Their father had gone to pieces.

But Nessa had been too young to do much but internalise all of her own pain and grief, too acutely aware of everyone else's struggles to let it out. She'd always been terrified of what might come out of her if she did. It had been easier to retreat emotionally, and concentrate on her dreams of being a great jockey.

But sometimes the pain in her chest—her unexpressed grief—took her breath away. And sometimes, when she looked at her sister Iseult with her husband and she saw their incredibly intimate bond, she felt envious of that relationship, even as it made her heart palpitate with fear. She couldn't imagine ever allowing herself to love someone that much, for fear of losing them. For fear of the devastation the loss would cause.

Up until now she'd avoided sex because getting close to someone had seemed like too high a price. And yet, when she thought of Luc Barbier, the last thing on her mind was the emotional price.

Luc was tired and frustrated. He'd spent the last three days working intensively with one of his brightest hopes, a horse called Sur La Mer. He was due to race in a few weeks in France but none of his jockeys seemed capable of getting the horse to perform to his maximum ability. Luc would ride the horse himself if he weren't six feet four and two hundred pounds.

Luc was also frustrated in a far more difficult area—sexually. It was not a state he was used to. He didn't do sexual frustration. He desired a woman, he had her and he moved on.

But only one woman had dominated his thoughts in France. Nessa O'Sullivan. He'd gone to a glitzy charity auction in Paris that was abounding with beautiful women. Not one had piqued his interest. Instead he'd found himself wondering what Nessa would look like out of those jeans that seemed to be shrink-wrapped to her taut thighs. Or the series of worn T-shirts that did little to conceal her lithe body and firm breasts. Or what her hair would look like teased into luxurious waves, rippling down a bare back.

Dieu. He cursed himself as he strode down the corridor to his bedroom, relishing the prospect of a cold shower and bed.

But when Luc opened the door to his bedroom all of his instincts snapped onto high alert. An old habit from when his environment had spelled danger from sunrise to sunset.

He saw the basket of cleaning supplies first, on a table near the door. And then he saw *her* and his breath stopped in his chest. He wasn't entirely sure he wasn't hallucinating.

She was curled up on the wide window seat, fast asleep. Her knees were leaning to one side, and her head was leaning against the window as if she'd been looking at the view of the gallops.

He moved closer and his hungry gaze tracked down over her body—he was disappointed that she wasn't wearing the jeans and T-shirt combination that had enflamed his imagination. She was wearing the plain black trousers and black shirt that all his household staff wore. Flat, functional sneakers.

The shirt had untucked from her trousers, and he could see the tiniest bare patch of her waist and her paler than pale skin. Blood roared to his head and groin in a simultaneous rush.

He was incensed at her effect on him, and at his growing obsession with her.

As if finally becoming aware of his intense scrutiny, she shifted slightly and Luc looked at her face to see long dark lashes fluttering against her cheeks for a moment before her eyes opened sleepily. He watched as she slowly registered where she was, and who was in front of her.

Her cheeks flushed and those huge eyes widened until all he could see was dark, golden green. He wanted to slip right into those pools and lose himself...

A tumult raged inside him as she looked up and blinked innocently, as if butter wouldn't melt in her mouth. He might have almost believed for a second that she hadn't planned this little set-up.

'Well, well, well, what do we have here?' He looked her over slowly and thoroughly, fresh heat flooding his veins when he saw the thrust of her breasts against the shirt. It made his voice harsh. 'You would have been much more comfortable and made it easier for both of us if you'd stripped naked and waited in my bed.'

CHAPTER FOUR

NESSA LOOKED UP at Luc Barbier, who was towering over her with a dark scowl on his face and stubble on his jaw. For a blessed foggy moment, just before the adrenalin kicked in, his words hung harmlessly in the air between them.

His hair was tousled, as if he'd been running a hand through it, and he was wearing a white shirt, open at the neck, revealing a glimpse of dark skin. Awareness sizzled to life, infusing her with an urgency she felt only around him.

And then his words registered. It was like an electric shock or a slap across the face. Nessa was wide awake, and she scrambled off the window seat to stand on wobbly legs.

Her hair was coming loose from where it had been piled messily on her head to keep it out of the way. She was thoroughly rumpled, she smelled of cleaning products and he really thought…? Bile rose in her throat.

'How dare you insinuate such a thing?' Her voice

was scratchy from sleep and she was burningly aware—even as she said that—of how bad this looked. She cursed herself for allowing her weariness to get the better of her.

Luc's head reared back, arms folded across his chest. 'I walk into my bedroom and find a woman, pretending to be asleep, waiting for me...like I said, they're usually in my bed and wearing a lot less but the message is essentially the same. They're here for one thing.'

Nessa was speechless at his sheer arrogance. Eventually she managed to get out, through waves of indignation and far more disturbing physical reactions, 'Well, I hate to burst your ego bubble but that was the last thing on my mind. I was cleaning your room, then I sat down for a minute and I fell asleep. I apologise for that. But I did not come here to...to...'

He raised a brow. 'To seduce me?'

Before she could respond to that, he continued as if she hadn't spoken. 'I might as well tell you now that kinky role-play doesn't really do it for me. I'm a traditionalist that way. When I make love it's intense, thorough and without the need for embellishment.'

A flash of heat went up Nessa's spine to imagine just how intense his lovemaking would be. Little beads of sweat broke out between her breasts and in the small of her back. Anger rose too. Anger that it was him who was firing up all her nerve-endings.

'I am not here to *make love* with anyone. My only

crime was to fall asleep on the job and if you'll excuse me now I'll leave you in peace.'

She went to step away and out of his orbit but he caught her arm after muttering something that sounded very French and rude under his breath. His hand encircled her whole upper arm and his fingers were brushing the side of her breast. Nessa's pulse rocketed, and in the dim lights of the room— *night had fallen outside...just how long had she been asleep?*—all she could see were the forbiddingly gorgeous lines of Luc's face.

'Peace?' He almost spat the word out. 'I've had precious little peace since your brother absconded with one million euros and then his temptress of a sister turns up to play sidekick. Just what is your agenda, Nessa? What game are you playing here? Because I warn you now that you will get burned if you think you can play with me and get away with it.'

His dark intensity was totally intimidating, but somehow Nessa managed to pull her arm free and step away. Shakily she said, 'I'm not playing any games. I wouldn't know how. I really didn't come here with some nefarious intention to seduce you.'

She bit her lip to stop a semi-hysterical giggle from emerging. She wouldn't know how to seduce her way out of a paper bag, never mind a man like Luc Barbier. The very notion was ridiculous.

His mouth thinned. 'You really expect me to believe that you fell asleep like Sleeping Beauty in the fairy tale, waiting for her prince?'

Heat rushed into her cheeks—she *had* been mooning about his suite like some lovelorn teenager earlier. It wasn't like her at all. 'I don't believe in fairy tales,' she said stiffly. 'And don't worry, I know you're no prince.'

He put two hands on her arms now, swinging her around to face him properly. His eyes had turned to cold steel. 'What's that supposed to mean?'

'I...' Words got stuck in Nessa's throat. She couldn't seem to concentrate on anything but Luc's face above hers. The sensual lines were mesmerising. 'I didn't mean anything.'

Except she had, she realised. She'd just articulated it badly. This man was no prince, he was a marauding sultan, or a king. Uncultivated and suave all at once. Infinitely hard but also soft, as when he'd put a hand to his horse.

His mouth twisted. 'I might never be a prince, but you're in no position to look down on me, the sister of a common thief who thought she could seduce her way to paying back her brother's debt. Like I said, you could have saved a lot of conversation if you'd been waiting in my bed naked instead of playing out this elaborate charade of innocence.'

Nessa's hand had lifted and connected with Luc's cheek before she even realised what she'd done. Shock coursed through her system as the sting registered on her hand and Luc's face turned from the blow. All her anger drained away instantly.

He turned back slowly, face even darker now, a

livid handprint showing on his cheek. Horrified, Nessa used his name for the first time. 'Luc, I'm so sorry. But I didn't mean it like that, and Paddy's not a common thief. He's really not—'

'Stop talking, you little hellcat, I don't want to hear another word.' His voice was rough.

Before Nessa could even think of uttering another word, Luc had pulled her right into him, so that her body was welded to his. All she could feel was whip-cord strength and heat.

All she could see were his eyes, fathomless and like molten steel. She realised he was livid and yet she felt no fear. She only felt an intense excitement. She opened her mouth but he said, 'Not another word.'

And then his mouth covered hers, and words were the last thing on Nessa's mind as heat fused with white light and poured into every vein in her body to create a scorching trail of fire.

Shock rendered her helpless to Luc's savage sensuality and her own immediately rampant response.

Luc's arm went around her back, arching her into him even more, and his mouth began to move over hers. But this was no gentle exploration, and it left any other kisses she'd shared with boys in a far distant universe. This did not leave her cold, or unmoved. This was igniting her very soul.

It was mastery, pure and simple. And domination. And punishment. And yet despite all those things that should have had Nessa tensing and squirming to be free, she strained to be even closer, raising her arms to twine them about Luc's neck. If she could have climbed into his skin, she would have.

She opened her mouth under his, instinctively seeking a deeper kiss, wanting to taste him with every fibre of her being. His fingers threaded through her hair, catching her head, angling it so that he could give her exactly what she wanted, but on his terms.

He consumed her, demanding nothing less than total surrender, and Nessa knew only one thing: that she wanted to surrender, with no doubt or hesitation in her mind. It was as if every moment in her life had been building up to this conflagration.

She was drowning in liquid heat and could feel it, slippery, between her legs. Luc's mouth left hers and she heard a soft moan emanating from her mouth. He trailed kisses over her jaw and down her neck. Her head fell back, too heavy.

The only sounds in the room were harsh breathing and the *thump thump* of her heart. Luc's hand was on her shirt, deftly opening the buttons. Cool air hit her bare skin and her nipples drew into tight, hard points.

The world tipped on its axis and Nessa only realised moments later that Luc had sat down on the edge of the bed, bringing her with him so that now she sat on his lap. She was dizzy, and thought that this must be how it felt to be drunk: light-headed and euphoric.

He was pushing her shirt open, and she looked at

him and saw an almost feral expression on his face.
He cupped one of her lace-covered breasts. Breasts
that had always felt very inadequate to Nessa. But
now when she looked down she could see how she
perfectly filled his palm. As if she'd been made for
his hands alone.

He pulled down the lace cup, baring her flesh, and
she bit her lip to stop from moaning, pleading. His
thumb skated over one small hard nipple and it sent
electric shocks through her whole body.

He looked at her and smiled and Nessa realised
that he hadn't smiled at her once until now. And it
was as devastating as she'd suspected it might be.
Wicked, seductive, gorgeous and irresistible.

Lust and need cocooned them from reality, and
for one wild second Nessa could almost convince
herself that perhaps she was still asleep and this was
all just a very vivid dream.

But she knew it wasn't a dream, and she knew that
it was very important that she stand up and stop this.

Luc's head was dipping towards her breast and
Nessa had never wanted anything more than to surrender completely to this moment, but something
within her, some small sane voice, broke through.
She put her hands on Luc's shoulders and levered
herself off his lap, feeling like a foal trying to stand
for the first time.

Luc just looked at her as if he couldn't quite believe she'd moved away, and Nessa realised she was
half naked. She pulled at her shirt, scrambling to

do up at least one or two buttons. The bare flesh of her breast chafed against the material, sensitised by his touch.

She forced out, through the clamour of her own desire, 'I didn't come here for this. I really didn't.'

Luc's body was hard and throbbed with a need to claim and possess, things he'd never felt for a woman before. Nessa was looking at him with wide eyes and flushed cheeks, and hair coming loose.

I didn't come here for this. Something slid into Luc's mind: the very rogue possibility that she *had* just fallen asleep while on the job. And then he dismissed it. She was playing with him and he would not be manipulated like this. He'd already exposed himself far too much. And the fact that she'd been the one to pull away, signalling she was more in control than he was, was even more exposing.

Luc forced his blood to cool, and stood up in a fluid motion. Nessa took a step back. The thought that she was stepping back from him in case he touched her again sent something dark into his gut. And something far more unwelcome: a feeling of vulnerability, something that Luc had rejected long ago. He was invulnerable.

'Sleeping with me isn't going to improve your, or your brother's, situation. I told you already that I don't play games, Nessa, so unless you're willing to admit that we both want each other with no strings attached then get out of here.'

His voice was so cold and remote it skated over

Nessa's skin like ice. She hated his obvious cynicism, and wanted to deny his claim that she would manipulate him to gain favour for her brother, but self-preservation kicked in at the last moment. She fled, taking the basket of cleaning supplies with her.

When Nessa finally made it back to her room she closed the door behind her and rested against it. Her heart was still thumping out of time, and her whole body ached for a fulfilment she'd never needed before.

And she reeled with the knowledge that she'd almost lain back for Luc Barbier and handed him something she'd never handed anyone else. Her innocence. She'd almost tipped over the edge of allowing Luc to see her at her most vulnerable. A man who had shown her nothing but disdain and distrust.

Thank *God* she'd pulled back from the brink. She shivered now at the prospect of Luc looking at her when he'd discovered her virginity. She could already imagine the mocking look on his face, and how he would spurn her with disgust.

But then she thought of how he'd said, *Unless you're willing to admit we both want each other with no strings attached*, and she shivered again. But this time it wasn't with trepidation or humiliation. It was with an awful sense of illicit excitement.

Luc had turned the shower to cold, but that still hadn't cooled the lingering heat in his body. He couldn't believe how close he'd come to stripping Nessa O'Sullivan bare and taking her in a haze of lust.

She'd been the one to pull back. And even though Luc hadn't imagined the chemistry between them, it still got to him somewhere very vulnerable that she'd had more control than him.

He couldn't trust her, and yet he'd been about to sleep with her, complicating an already complicated situation even more. He shuddered to think of the hold she could have had over him after sleeping together. He hadn't yet known a woman who didn't try to capitalise on intimacies shared, even when they were only physical. And he had no doubt—in spite of her protestations otherwise—that she'd had an agenda.

He looked at himself in his bathroom mirror and scowled. If she thought that she could whet his appetite like this, and he would come running after her like a dog in heat, she was mistaken. Luc wouldn't be caught offguard again. She *was* resistable. Even if the pounding of his blood told him otherwise.

He pulled a towel around his waist and knotted it roughly, finding his mobile phone and picking it up. Within seconds he was issuing a terse instruction to the security firm he'd hired to seek out Paddy O'Sullivan, to step up their efforts.

Afterwards he threw the phone down and surmised grimly that the sooner they found Paddy and his money, the sooner he could get rid of the all too distracting Nessa O'Sullivan too.

Two nights later, Nessa was holding a tray full of champagne flutes filled to the brim, serving them at Luc's glitzy party. She was dressed in a white shirt and black skirt. The uniform of waiters everywhere. Hair up in a tight bun.

She could appreciate the breathtaking scene even as her arms felt as if they were about to drop out of the shoulder sockets. The unusually mild Irish spring day was melting into a lavender-hued dusk. Candles imbued the guests and room with a golden light.

She smiled in relief as some guests stopped and helped themselves to drinks on her tray, lightening her load marginally. And then her gaze tracked back inevitably to where one man stood out from the crowd—dark head and broad shoulders visible from every corner of the room.

Her main objective was to avoid coming face to face with Luc Barbier at all costs. The enormity of what had almost happened still sent shock waves through her body every time she thought of it. *So did the thought of a no-strings encounter,* added a wicked voice.

And even though she was trying to avoid him, she couldn't look away. Much like most of the women in the room, she'd noticed with a spurt of something suspiciously…possessive. He was dressed in a tuxedo and he was simply breathtaking. He was the epitome of virile beauty, but with that undeniable edge of something dark and dangerous.

As if reading her mind, two women stopped nearby and, in that way of seeing but not seeing Nessa, because she was staff, they were whispering loudly enough for Nessa to catch snippets.

'Apparently he's an animal in bed...'

'They say he was found on the streets...'

'Petty crime...'

'Only got to where he has because he slept with Leo Fouret's wife and the husband bought him off to keep him quiet...'

Nessa went still at that, something cold trickling down her spine. She hadn't heard that final, particular rumour before. Although, he *had* apparently left Leo Fouret's stables under less than amicable circumstances, before blazing a trail on his own.

The women moved away and then more guests approached Nessa, relieving her of her remaining drinks. She was only too happy to escape back to the kitchen to stock up. Just before she left, she cast one last glance in Luc's direction, but his head was bowed towards someone in conversation.

Lambasting herself for having listened to gossip, no matter how inadvertently, Nessa forged a path through the crowd and away from Luc. She told herself that she wasn't remotely interested in what the women had been saying. And that she was truly pathetic to be feeling the tiniest bit sorry for him that he was surrounded by such fervent gossip in the first place.

There was no smoke without a fire, as her father loved to say on a regular basis. And from what she'd seen of Luc in action, she could almost forgive a married woman for falling under his spell.

'What on earth is Nessa O'Sullivan doing serving drinks at your party, Barbier? I'd hardly think she's short of a few bob!'

It took a second for Luc to register what the man beside him had said and when he did his wandering attention snapped into sharp focus. 'You know her?'

The man snorted. 'Of course I do you forget Ireland is a small place. Her father is Paddy O'Sullivan, one of this country's best trainers—at one time. Before he hit the bottle and almost lost everything. Now of course they're back on top of the world, although I don't think Paddy will ever repair the damage to his reputation. Still, he doesn't need to now, not with the goldmine he's sitting on thanks to his son-in-law.'

Luc usually had an aversion to gossip but not this time. 'What are you talking about?'

Percy Mortimer, a well-known English racing pundit, turned to Luc. 'Nessa O'Sullivan is related to royalty—her older sister—who incidentally is also a very talented amateur trainer—is married to the supreme Sheikh Nadim Al-Saqr of Merkazad. He bought out their stud a few years back. Nessa's not a bad rider. I've seen her in a couple of races over the years, but she doesn't seem to have made a proper impression yet.'

What the hell? Luc barely heard that last bit. Sheikh Nadim was a very serious contender in racing circles, and a billionaire. And Luc had had no idea that he owned a stables just down the road. *Nessa's family stud.* He reeled, although he didn't show it.

Percy was saying something else but Luc wasn't listening. His gaze was already scanning the crowd for a dark redhead. He'd seen her earlier—looking once again as if butter wouldn't melt, dressed in her white shirt and skirt. Even that small glimpse had been enough to cause a spike in his heart-rate.

Damn. Where was she, anyway?

Luc tried to move away but saw a group headed for him with Pascal leading the way. The look on Pascal's face told Luc that he had to stay exactly where he was.

Nessa would have to wait, for now. But he would track her down and this time there would be no games. Only answers to his questions. Like what the hell was she playing at, working for nothing to pay off her brother's debt when presumably she could ask for a handout from her billionaire brother-in-law?

Nessa's feet and arms were aching, and she knew she shouldn't be here, but after the party had finished and they'd been released, she found herself gravitating towards the stallions' stables. As if pulled by some magnetic force. As if that could help to ground her and fuse her scattered energies back together.

She'd been acutely conscious of Luc's every movement, all evening.

At one stage she'd caught his eye and it had seemed as if he was trying to communicate something telepathically. From the grim look on his face it hadn't been something particularly nice. And then, even though she'd skirted around the edges of the room, keeping far out of his orbit for the rest of the evening, she could have sworn she felt his dark gaze boring into her periodically.

She came to a stop in the middle of the stables when she realised that they were empty. She looked around and remembered belatedly that the stallions had been moved up to different paddocks and stables for a few days while these were being repainted and renovated.

There were white sheets piled high in a corner along with painting and cleaning paraphernalia. Nessa told herself it was just as well as she turned around to leave. The last thing she needed was to be caught again in the wrong place—

Her heart stopped when she saw the tall broad figure blocking the doorway, with only the moon behind him as a silhouette. Too late. *Luc*.

She could see that his bow-tie was undone and top button open, his jacket swinging loose and his hands in the pockets of his trousers.

He moved forward into the stables and she saw

his stern expression revealed in the dim lighting. Immediately the space felt claustrophobic. Nessa's body tingled with awareness as he came close enough for her to see that there was also barely leashed anger in his expression.

She swallowed. 'I know I shouldn't be here—'

'That's not important. We need to have a little chat.'

Surprise robbed her voice for a moment and then she said, 'About what?'

Luc folded his arms. 'About why you've omitted to mention the not inconsequential fact that your sister is married to Sheikh Nadim Al-Saqr of Merkazad, *and* that he owns your stud farm.'

He continued, 'I'd imagine one million euro is short change to Sheikh Nadim Al-Saqr, so what the hell is Paddy doing jeopardising his career for a handout he could've begged off his brother-in-law, and why didn't *you* just pick up the phone to Nadim to sort this mess out?'

Nessa went hot and then cold as the significance of this sank in, and the realisation that someone must have recognised her at the party.

She said carefully, 'I didn't think it was relevant.'

Luc looked even more stern. 'Not good enough.'

Nessa swallowed. She knew she couldn't avoid an explanation. 'Nadim *did* buy our farm but he put it back into our name as a wedding gift for Iseult, my sister. It's ours again, he's just one of the shareholders. And I didn't want to involve him because this has nothing to do with Nadim or Iseult. My sister is due to have a baby in a couple of weeks and they don't need the stress.'

Luc stepped closer but Nessa was trapped, with a stable door at her back and nowhere to go. She was acutely aware of his tall, lean body and his scent.

'There's more to it than that,' he said. 'You and your brother avoiding asking for help just proves you're both involved in something that's gone beyond your control. I'm guessing Nadim wouldn't approve, and you don't want to bite the hand that feeds you.'

In a fierce low voice Nessa replied, '*No.* It's nothing like that. Why must you be so cynical and mistrustful?'

'Because,' he answered smoothly, 'I was born that way and nothing I've experienced has ever proved me wrong. Life favours the opportunistic. I should know.'

I was born that way. Nessa couldn't stop a rush of curiosity and pity. The second time she'd pitied him this evening. But then she crushed it. Luc Barbier was the last man on the planet who needed anyone's pity.

He said, 'You could be free to walk away if you asked Nadim for help.'

Luc heard himself say the words even as something inside him rejected it immediately. Let her walk away? A hot surge of possessiveness rose up inside him. *He wanted her.*

She was looking at him, eyes huge, and for a second he could almost have imagined that she looked... *hurt*. A ridiculous notion.

Nessa shook her head and some long tendrils of red hair framed her face. 'No. I will not take the easy way out and cause my family distress. I promised Paddy that I wouldn't go to Nadim or Iseult.'

Luc was intrigued by this apparent loyalty. 'Give me one good reason why I shouldn't go to Nadim myself.'

An expression of panic crossed her face. 'I thought you didn't want this news to get out either!'

'I don't. But from what I know of the Sheikh, I think he would appreciate the need for discretion on his family's behalf. It would affect his name and reputation too.'

Nessa wrung her hands in front of her and it only drew Luc's attention to where the shirt strained slightly over her breasts. He dragged his gaze up.

'You have no right to involve them.'

Now he really wanted to know why she was being so stubborn on this. 'Give me one reason, Nessa, and make it a good one.'

She looked at him as if he was torturing her and then she answered with palpable reluctance. 'When our mother died Iseult was only twelve; I was eight. Our father couldn't cope with the grief. He went off the rails, and developed a drink problem. Iseult went to school, but she did the bare minimum so that she could take care of the farm, the horses and all of us.'

Nessa glanced away for a moment, her face pale. Luc felt at an uncharacteristic loss as to what to say but she looked back at him and continued. 'If it wasn't for Iseult shielding us from the worst of our father's excesses and the reality of the farm falling to pieces, we never would have made it through school. She shouldered far too much for someone her age...and then Nadim came along and bought the farm out and she felt as if she'd failed us all at the last hurdle.'

Nessa drew in a breath. 'But then they fell in love and got married, and for the first time in her life she's really secure and happy.'

'Married to a billionaire, conveniently enough.' The cynical comment was said before Luc had even properly thought about it, and it felt hollow on his lips.

Nessa's hands clenched to fists by her sides. 'Iseult is the least materialistic person I know. They love each other.'

Luc was a bit stunned by her vehemence. 'Go on.'

She bit her lip for a moment, and he had to stop himself from reaching out to tug it free of those small white teeth.

'My sister is truly happy for the first time in a long time. The only responsibility she now bears is to her own family. They had problems getting pregnant after Kamil so this pregnancy has been stressful. If she knew what was going on she'd be devastated and worried, and Nadim would do everything he could to help her. He might even insist on coming all the way over here, and she needs him with her now.'

She added impetuously, 'If you do talk to Nadim, I'll leak it to the press about the money going astray. Maybe they'll be easier on Paddy than you've been.'

Luc just looked at Nessa for a long moment, and he had to admit with grudging reluctance that her apparent zeal to protect her family was very convincing. He'd never seen a mother bear with cubs, but he had an impression of it right now. And he didn't like how it had affected him when she'd mentioned her sister's happy family. For a second he'd actually felt something like envy.

It reminded him uncomfortably of when he'd been much younger and he and other kids from the flats would go into Paris to pick pockets or whatever petty crime they could get away with. Stupid kids with nothing to lose and no one at home to care what they got up to.

One day Luc had been mesmerised by a family playing in a park—a mother, father and two children. The kids had looked so happy and loved. An awful darkness had welled up inside him and he'd tasted jealousy for the first time. And something far more poignant—a desire to know what that would be like.

His friends had noticed and had teased Luc unmercifully, so he'd shoved that experience and those feelings deep down inside and had vowed never to envy anyone again. And he wasn't about to start now.

But eclipsing all of that now was the carnal hunger building inside him. He'd thought of little else but that incendiary kiss the other night. When he'd sought Nessa out after the party he'd told himself he could resist her. But the thick sexual tension in the air mocked him.

She called to him, even in those plain, unerotic clothes. She called to him, deep inside where a dark hunger raged and begged for satisfaction.

Suddenly it didn't matter who she was related to. Or if she was playing mind-games. She threw up too many questions, but there was only one question he was interested in knowing the answer to right now, and that was how she would feel when he sank deep inside her.

Luc closed the distance between them, and reached out to slide a hand around Nessa's neck, tugging her closer. Her eyes went wide and her cheeks bloomed with colour. She put a hand up to his and said, 'What are you doing?'

Luc's gaze was fixated on her mouth and he had to drag it away to look into those huge hazel eyes. 'Do you really expect me to believe that you're just an innocent who would do anything for her family? And that the other night was pure chance and chemistry?'

For a taut moment, Luc held his breath because he realised that some small kernel of the little boy he'd once been, yearning for something totally out of his orbit, was still alive inside him. He waited for Nessa to gaze up at him with those huge eyes and move closer, to tell him in a husky voice, *Yes, I'm really that innocent.* The worst of it was, he wasn't entirely sure that he wouldn't believe her.

But she didn't. She tensed and pulled back, jerking free of Luc's hand. Glaring up at him. 'I don't *expect* you to believe anything, Luc Barbier. You've got eyes in your head and if you choose to view the world through a fog of cynicism and mistrust then that's your prerogative.

'As for the other night—it was madness and a mistake. You won't have to worry why it happened because it won't happen again.'

Nessa had almost moved past Luc when his shocked brain kicked into gear and he caught her hand, stopping her. Every cell in his body rejected what she'd just said. She was walking away again. A savage part of himself rose up, needing to prove that she wasn't as in control as she appeared.

He pulled her back in front of him. 'You want me.'

She bit her lip and looked down. She shook her head. Luc tipped her chin up feeling even more savage. 'Say it, Nessa.'

She looked at him, eyes huge and swirling with emotion but Luc couldn't draw back now. Eventually she said with a touch of defiance, 'I might want you but I don't want to.'

Something immediately eased inside him. She glanced down again as if by not looking at him she could avoid the issue.

'Look at me, Nessa.'

For a long moment she refused but then she looked

up, eyes spitting golden sparks, and it ignited the fire inside him to a burning inferno of need. He pulled her closer again. She put her hands up to his chest. 'No, Luc. I don't want—'

But he stopped her words with his mouth and used every ounce of his expertise to show her how futile her resistance was. Whatever else was happening around them, whatever she was saying, he could trust that this was true at least.

CHAPTER FIVE

NESSA WANTED TO resist Luc—she really did. She hated that he still patently believed she'd orchestrated the other night. And that he most likely didn't believe what she'd told him about her family.

But it was hard to think of all of that when his mouth was on hers and he was sliding his tongue between her lips and possessing her with such devastating ease. Big hands moved down her back to her buttocks, cupping them and bringing her in close to where she could feel the bold thrust of his arousal. For her. Not for one of the stunningly beautiful women at the party. *Her.* Nessa O'Sullivan.

He drew back then and Nessa realised she was welded to him. Arms and breasts crushed against his chest. One arm kept her clamped to him, not letting her escape for a moment. He undid her hair so that it fell around her shoulders. He looked at it for a moment as if mesmerised and something inside Nessa melted.

He wrapped some hair around his hand and gently tugged so that her head came back. And then he kissed her again, dragging her deeper and deeper into the pit of a fire that she knew she couldn't walk away from again. She'd barely been able to the last time.

He pulled her skirt up until she felt cool air skate over her heated skin. He palmed the flesh of her buttocks and the place between her legs burned with damp heat.

She broke away from the kiss, breathing rapidly, and looked at him. Her heart was racing. She couldn't look away from his eyes. They held her to account and she couldn't lie.

'What do you want, Nessa?' His fingers moved tantalisingly close to the edge of her panties. Her breathing quickened. One finger slid under the material, stroking. Her legs were weak.

'Do you want me to stop?'

No! shouted every fibre of her being. Nessa couldn't explain it and wasn't sure if she even wanted to investigate it, but she realised at that moment that she trusted him. She wasn't sure *what* she trusted exactly. Maybe it was that he wouldn't lie to her or spout platitudes. And so she convinced herself that if she said yes to this…whatever it was…she'd be under no illusions that emotions were involved.

He drew back marginally. 'Nessa?' And there it was—a glimmer of concern, showing a side to this darkly complex man that she suspected not many people ever got to see. She knew he would let her go if she insisted, even if his pride demanded her capitulation. Even as they both knew she would capitulate all too easily. But, she wanted this man with every cell in her body. She'd never wanted anything as much.

'Don't stop,' she whispered, reaching up to wind her arms around his neck again, pressing her mouth to his. Luc didn't hesitate. He gathered her even closer and backed her into the stall behind them, where she'd seen all the white sheets piled up in readiness for the work.

Nessa felt a soft surface at the backs of her legs that swiftly gave way, and she fell into the pile of sheets.

Luc looked down at Nessa, sprawled before him. Her skirt was up around her smooth thighs, and her untucked shirt strained across her chest. Her red hair spilled across the white fabric. It was probably one of the least romantic settings for lovemaking, but it was one of the most erotic sights Luc had ever seen. He was no longer aware of anything but the pounding in his blood and the need he felt in every cell of his body.

A small voice tried to get through to him, to remind him that he was no longer this uncivilised man, but it fell on deaf ears as he started to take off his clothes with the singular intention of joining their naked bodies as soon as possible.

Nessa stared up at Luc. The intense expression on his face might have scared her if she didn't feel as though she might have a similar expression on her face. He pulled off his jacket, dropping it to the ground, and then his bow tie. He started to open his shirt and Nessa's eyes grew wide as his magnificent chest was revealed bit by glorious bit until he was naked from the waist up. She could hardly breathe.

He came down over her, arms bracketing around her body, and his head dipped to hers, mouths fusing again in a series of long, drugging kisses that made Nessa want more, much more.

By the time he was opening her shirt, she was arching her back towards him in silent supplication. He pushed apart the material and pulled down the lace cups of her bra, exposing her breasts to his dark gaze as he rested on one arm beside her.

'*Si belle...*' he murmured before dipping his head and surrounding one tight peak in wet heat. Nessa might have screamed, she wasn't sure. She just knew that Luc's mouth on her bare flesh was almost more than she could bear. And he was remorseless, ignoring her pleas for mercy.

His mouth moved down over her belly, and he pulled up her skirt so that it was ruched around her waist. He stopped for a moment and looked at her in the dim light, watching her expression as his hand explored under the waist of her panties before gently pushing them down her legs.

Nessa sucked in a breath. This was more exposed than she'd ever been in her life, and yet it didn't scare her. She felt exhilarated.

Luc's gaze moved down her body and his hand rested between her legs, cupping her. Slowly, he started to move his hand against her and Nessa gripped his arms like an anchor.

He watched her again as one finger explored in a circle, through her secret folds of flesh and then right into the heart of her. Nessa's back arched and she squeezed her eyes shut. It was sensory overload. Her legs were splayed and Luc's hand was a wicked instrument of torture, as one finger became two, stretching her.

She lifted her head. 'I can't…' Was that her voice? So needy and husky?

'Can't what, *chérie*?'

'Can't cope…what you're doing, it's too much…'

He smiled and it was the smile of the devil. 'It's not nearly enough. *Yet.* Come fly with me, *minou.* Come on…'

She didn't understand what he was asking, but then he flicked his finger against the very heart of her. She tumbled blindly over an edge she had no chance of saving herself from.

If Luc had ever wanted to assert his dominance, he just had. With pathetic ease.

It took a long moment for Nessa to come back to her senses. She felt undone but deliciously sated. And yet there was something deeper, throbbing with need inside her, an instinctive knowledge of something even greater to come.

'*Ca va?*'

Nessa opened her eyes to see Luc looking at her. If he'd looked smug or remotely triumphant she might have wakened from this craziness but he didn't. He looked slightly...fascinated.

She nodded. She didn't know what she was but it was better than *okay*.

Luc's hand moved up to cup her breast, fingers finding and pinching her nipple lightly. Immediately her body was humming again, as if she hadn't just orgasmed.

She realised that Luc's chest was within touching distance and reached out shyly to touch him. Tentative, but growing more adventurous when she felt how warm he was, and the latent steel of his body underneath.

'You really don't have to pretend, *minou*.'

He sounded slightly amused. Nessa's hand stopped and she looked at him. 'Pretend...what are you talking about?'

'Pretend to be some kind of innocent. I told you I don't get off on games. It's really not necessary. I want you, more than I've ever wanted anyone else.'

She wasn't pretending; she *was* innocent! His face suddenly looked stark, as if he hadn't meant to say those words, and treacherously it robbed her of any words of defence. Somehow she knew that if she said anything, this would all stop and she wasn't ready for it to be over.

So she did the most selfish thing she'd ever done in her life and said nothing. She touched him again, placing her mouth over his blunt nipples and exploring with her tongue, feeling ridiculously powerful when she heard him hiss between his teeth and felt him catch her hair again, winding it around his hand as if he needed to restrain her.

It was an incredible aphrodisiac to know she had any kind of effect on Luc Barbier.

She explored further, down his body, tracing her fingers over abs so tight that her own quivered in response. And then she reached his belt. There was a moment, and then he said gruffly, 'Keep going.'

So she undid the belt, sliding it through the loops, then his button and the zip. She could feel the potent thrusting bulge under the material and her hand started to shake as she drew the zip down.

Luc muttered something in French and then he was standing up and pushing his trousers down and off, taking his underwear with them. And now he was naked and fully aroused and Nessa couldn't speak, taking in his virile majesty.

'Touch me.'

Nessa sat up and reached out, curling her hand tentatively around Luc's rigid erection. She found it fascinating—the silky skin pulled taut over all that potent strength. There was a bead of moisture at the top, and, acting completely on instinct, she leant over and touched it with her tongue, tasting the tart saltiness. Her mouth watered and she wanted to wrap her whole mouth around him but he was pulling her away saying, 'Stop…or I won't last.'

Luc's brain was so fused with lust and heat and need that it was all he could do not to thrust between the tempting lushness of Nessa's lips. All rational thought had gone. He couldn't wait. He needed to feel her whole body around him, not just her mouth.

He moved over her, between her spread legs, and for a second the way she was looking up at him, with some expression he'd never seen on a woman's face before, almost made him stop, and take a breath. This was too crazy. Too rushed. He needed to get his wits back...

But then he felt her hands on his hips as if guiding him into her and he was lost again, drowning in need.

Nessa was filled with a raw sense of earthy urgency so sharp and intense she found herself reaching for Luc, wanting to bring him closer. He knelt between her legs, spreading them wider with his hands.

Nessa was vaguely aware that her shirt was open, her breasts bared and her skirt ruched around her waist. But any selfconsciousness fled when the head of his erection nudged against where she was so hot and wet. She instinctively circled her hips up to meet him.

Nothing could have prepared her though for that first cataclysmic penetration. She felt impaled. Luc was too big. He looked at her for a moment with a line between his brows and her heart stopped. *Did he know?* But then he slid in a little further. The discomfort faded as he filled her more, all the way until she couldn't breathe.

As he started to move in and out he lifted her leg and wrapped it around his hip, making him move even deeper inside her. Nessa was clasping his shoulders, needing something to hold onto as tension wound into a tight ball deep inside her.

She'd never felt anything like the glorious glide of his body in and out of hers. She was utterly consumed with the moment and what this man was doing to her.

She wrapped both legs around him now, digging her heels into his buttocks, wanting, needing more. Sweat made their skin glisten and their breathing was harsh as they both raced to the pinnacle of the climb.

Luc's movements became faster and Nessa could only cling on for dear life as the oncoming storm hurtled towards her. He arched her up towards him and found a nipple with his hot mouth, sucking it deep, and at that moment Nessa was flung into the eye of the storm and she cried out a release that went on, and on, and on.

Luc went taut above her and she felt the warm rush of his release inside her but at that point her brain was too burnt out to think of anything else but the oblivion that extreme pleasure brought in its wake.

After a long moment, with Luc's body embedded in hers, Nessa felt as if she were claiming him. Immediately she rejected it as a ridiculous notion. Luc

Barbier was not a man who would ever be claimed. That much was obvious.

She unlocked her arms from around his neck. His breath was warm against her neck. He moved then and she winced as tender muscles protested. He didn't look at her as he pulled away and stood up.

Nessa felt self-conscious and realised how wanton she must look, spreadeagled and with her clothes in total disarray. She started to pull her shirt back over her chest, and her skirt down, feeling cold. She had no idea how to behave in this unorthodox and totally new situation to her—post-sex etiquette. In a stables. On sheets.

Luc was just standing there, half turned away, like a statue. Nessa's hands stilled and she came up on one elbow. Something caught her attention, a long angry scar that zigzagged down Luc's back. She remembered feeling it under her hand in the throes of passion. But it hadn't registered fully.

She sat up. 'What is that on your back?'

Finally, he looked at her and his face was expressionless. Little alarm bells went off.

'My scar?'

She nodded, horrified to imagine him suffering such violence.

'It's a reminder from a long time ago to not forget who I am or where I came from.'

Nessa didn't like how it almost sounded like a warning. 'That sounds serious.'

Luc looked at her. 'My scar isn't serious. What is serious is that we didn't use protection.'

Nessa insides seized with icy panic when she remembered feeling the warm rush of his release. How could she have let that happen?

And then she ordered her sluggish brain to kick into gear and breathed a sigh of relief, tinged with something much more disturbing, like regret. Which was crazy. After her experience losing her mother, Nessa had never relished the prospect of becoming a mother that could die and potentially devastate her family. No matter how cute her little nephew was, or how envious she felt when she saw his special bond with her sister.

She'd taken birth control in college but had stopped soon after leaving, not deeming it necessary when it had never been necessary there. Now she felt supremely naive and foolish.

She forced herself to look at Luc. 'I'm at a safe place in my cycle.'

Luc made a mirthless, almost bitter sound. 'I'm supposed to take your word for it?'

Anger surged at herself for being so lax and at his accusatory tone. She stood up, pulling her shirt together and her skirt down, hair wild and loose. She mustered up every atom of dignity she could given the circumstances and said coolly, 'Well, you'll have to just take my word for it. There were two of us involved, so why weren't *you* thinking of protection?'

* * *

Because for the first time in a long time he'd been a slave to his base desires, and protection had been the last thing on his mind.

The realisation sent shards of jagged panic into Luc's guts. How could he have forgotten one of his most stringent rules? He, who had vowed never to have children because he had no desire for a family. Family was anathema to him. And to forget that with this woman, of all women? She was the one most likely to turn around now and use this for her own gain. He might as well have just handed her a loaded gun.

Except even now, Luc was still acutely aware of Nessa's state of déshabillé and how much he wanted to tip her back onto the sheets and take her again. He reached for his trousers, pulling them on angrily, disgusted with his lack of self-control.

He was in the grip of a tumult inside him that he didn't know how to decipher or necessarily want to. All he knew was that what had just happened between him and this woman left anything else he'd ever experienced in the dust. It hadn't just been mind-blowing sex. It had been something else. Something that had affected him on another level.

More disgust ran through him—he'd just done what he expressly forbade his own employees from doing. And now he'd made things exponentially worse by not using protection.

Nessa was looking at him and he realised she was

pale. He knew he was being a bastard—it had been his responsibility to protect them. Not hers. He ran a hand through his hair. 'Look, I'm sorry. I just… I don't ever forget about something as fundamental as protection.'

She still looked pale and his chest felt tight. 'What's wrong?' *Had he hurt her?* He was so much bigger than her and the last thing on his mind had been taking care, or being gentle.

What's wrong? What's right? Nessa glanced away for a moment feeling ridiculously vulnerable, and even more so after his apology. She hadn't expected cuddles and a heart-to-heart after sex with this man—no matter how much lust had clouded her brain. But she also hadn't expected him to be so obviously angry with himself.

He hadn't even noticed that she was a virgin. He'd thought she was acting innocent.

She forced herself to look at him and for a second could have almost imagined she'd dreamed up the last hour. He was dressed again, albeit without his tie and jacket. She still felt thoroughly dishevelled and at a disadvantage, and suddenly she wanted to pierce that cool disdain and self-recrimination.

'I don't know what this is between us but I'm not proud of myself,' she said.

Luc looked at her with no discernible change in his expression, but then she saw the merest flash of something almost like hurt cross his face. He stepped closer, and she could see his eyes burning and a muscle jumping in his jaw.

'You might be related to royalty but if you were seated at a banquet table right now and dressed head to toe in couture, you would still want me. Lust makes great levellers of all of us. As does crime,' he answered.

It took a second for Nessa to absorb what he'd said. She couldn't believe he'd misunderstood her. He turned away at that moment and, in spite of the turmoil she was feeling, she reached out, wrapping a hand around his arm. 'Stop.'

He turned around.

She swallowed. 'I didn't mean that I wasn't proud because it was *you*. I meant that I'm not proud because I feel like I'm betraying my family.'

His lip curled. 'It's just sex, Nessa. Don't overthink it.'

She immediately felt silly for opening her mouth. She let his arm go and stepped back. 'Forget I said anything.'

She was about to step around him and make her exit to lick her wounds and castigate herself for being so weak but this time he took her arm, stopping her and asking harshly, 'What is that?'

Nessa looked around and for a second couldn't see what he was looking at behind them. But then she noticed the unmistakable stain of red on the white sheets. Her blood. Her virginal blood.

She went icy cold, and then hot with humiliation. Quickly she stood in front of it. 'It's nothing.'

He moved her aside and looked closer. If the ground could have opened up and swallowed Nessa whole she would have jumped right in.

He looked at it for so long Nessa wished she'd taken the chance to escape. But then he moved back, and there was such a mix of expressions on his face that she was stunned into silence.

Luc couldn't believe what his eyes had just told him, and yet he couldn't stop thinking about all the moments when he'd thought she was putting on some act with the shy tentative kisses, the self-consciousness, and the way she'd run the other night.

But what beat at his brain most of all had been that moment, when he'd felt her body clamping tight around him. It had made him stop, and look at her, but the question had barely formed in his mind before her muscles had been relaxing to let him go deeper, and he'd conveniently blocked the half-formed question out, too desperate to sate himself.

She'd been a *virgin*.

That knowledge filled him with too many things to untangle now. One of which was a fierce feeling of satisfaction that he'd been her first. It was something he'd never imagined feeling in a scenario like this.

'Why didn't you tell me?'

She opened her mouth and closed it again, and that only brought Luc's attention to those lush lips and how they'd felt on his body.

'Well?' he snapped. She flinched minutely and Luc bit back a curse at himself. He felt unmoored, boorish. Out of control.

A hint of defiance came into her eyes and it comforted him. This woman was no wilting lily.

'I didn't think it was relevant. Or that you'd notice.'

Luc burned inside at that. He had noticed but had dismissed it. 'I don't sleep with virgins.'

Nessa folded her arms and said tartly, 'Well, you just did.'

He felt the burn of more self-recrimination. 'If I'd known I wouldn't have been so...rough.'

Amazingly, Nessa blushed and glanced away. 'You weren't too rough.' She hesitated. 'It was okay.'

'Okay?'

She looked back at him. 'I mean, I don't know, do I? It was my first time.'

Her words propelled Luc forward and he caught her arms in his hands. She felt unbearably slender and delicate all of a sudden. He was acutely aware of how petite she was. 'It was more than *okay*. I felt your body's response, and not everyone has that experience for their first time.'

She blushed even more now but she stared at him. 'I'll have to take your word for it.'

Luc was torn between laughing out loud at her sheer front and tipping her back onto the sheets to remind her exactly how unbelievably good it had been. But she'd be sore, and frankly he didn't like the strength of the emotions running through him. This was not a post-sex scenario he had ever experienced before. Usually there was a bare minimum of conversation before he left. Right now it was hard to let her go.

In fact, he was afraid that the longer they stood there, the more likely it was that he *would* take her again. Especially when she was looking at him with those huge pools of amber and green. Her face flushed and hair wild. Clothes in disarray.

Doing something he'd never done before— exhibiting any kind of post-sex tenderness—he put his hands to the buttons of her shirt and did them up, gritting his jaw when he felt the swells of her breasts underneath the material.

He stood back. 'You should go. Take a bath. You'll be tender.'

She swallowed and for a moment looked endearingly unsure. And unbelievably sexy.

'*Go*, Nessa,' Luc growled, aware of the tenuous grip on his control.

She looked around at the sheet and made a gesture. 'I should take—'

'I'll take care of it.' This was unprecedented territory for Luc.

Finally, she left and Luc watched her walk out, slightly unsteadily. Her skirt was still at an angle and all he could see were those slim legs and remember how they'd felt clamped around his hips. She was a lot stronger than she looked.

Luc tried to make sense of what had just happened but it was hard. One thing was sure, though: Nessa O'Sullivan had just managed to impact somewhere no one had touched him in a long, long time. And if he was to consciously allow her to gain any more advantage, then he'd be the biggest fool. What just happened…it couldn't happen again. No matter how much he wanted her.

Nessa stayed in the bath until the water cooled and her skin had started to pucker. There was tenderness between her legs but also a lingering buzz of pleasure.

She couldn't quite believe the sequence of events that had led to that frantic coupling on sheets in a stables with Luc Barbier.

Her whole body got hot just recalling how quickly they'd combusted. How easily she'd given in, and given away her innocence. And, how easily she'd justified it to herself. *And you'd do it again right now if you could*, whispered a wicked little voice. Nessa knew it was true. She wouldn't have the strength to resist Luc again, not after that. It was like experiencing paradise and then having to deny it existed.

And while he wasn't here right now, cosseting her and whispering sweet nothings in her ear, the way he'd told her to leave and take a bath, and how he'd done up her buttons for her, had made her feel pathetically cared for.

She cringed and wanted to submerge herself under

the water when she thought of how Luc had to be seriously regretting what had happened. Nessa cringed even more to think of him disposing of the evidence of her virginity.

He was a man used to sleeping with the most beautiful women in the world: experienced worldly women, not naive innocents like Nessa.

She took a deep breath as if testing for emotional pain and she let it out shakily. Her emotions were intact. Luc had impacted her on a physical level but that was all, she assured herself.

Liar, mocked a voice. Seeing those slivers of the more complex man under his stern exterior, and his gruffly tender treatment at the end had moved her more than she cared to admit.

If she saw any more evidence of *that* Luc, she wasn't so sure her emotions would remain untouched. And forming an attachment to Luc Barbier would be a lesson in futility and pain. Of that she was certain.

One thing was clear. The moment of madness just now couldn't happen again. Not that Nessa imagined for a second that Luc wanted it to. His self-recrimination had been palpable, and that suited Nessa fine. *It did*, she told herself. No matter what her newly awakened body might be aching for in secret places.

CHAPTER SIX

LUC LOOKED AT the figure riding the horse and couldn't believe what he was seeing. The boy—for it had to be a boy, he was too slight to be a man— was riding one of his prize thoroughbreds as if he'd been riding her all his life.

Jockey and horse were one entity, cutting through the air like a bullet. He'd never seen the filly perform so well. And he already itched to see what the jockey would be like on Sur La Mer, back in France. He just knew instinctively that he could be the missing link to get the best out of the horse.

Luc looked at his chief Irish trainer. 'Okay, who is he and where has he been before now, and can we retain him immediately?' Luc knew how rare it was to find raw talent like this.

Pete had come to him a few minutes ago and just said enigmatically, *You need to see this.*

Pete grinned. 'He's a *she*.'

'What the—?' Luc looked back and his skin prick- led with a kind of awareness. The jockey and horse came around the nearest corner and as they thundered past him he caught a glimpse of dark red hair tucked under the cap and a delicate jawline. He recalled Percy Mortimer saying Nessa was a good rider.

Luc's nervous system fizzed immediately, even before Pete said, 'It's Nessa O'Sullivan.'

For the past couple of days Luc had been ruthlessly crushing any memories or reminders of what had happened in the stables. At night, though, when he was asleep, he couldn't control his mind: his dreams were filled with X-rated memories. He'd woken every morning with a throbbing erection and every muscle screaming for release.

He hadn't been at the mercy of his body like this since his hormones had run wild as a teenager.

It was galling; humiliating.

And here she was again, provoking him.

Pete was looking at him. 'Well?'

Luc controlled himself with effort. 'What the hell is she doing on my horse?'

Pete's grin faded. He put up his hands in a gesture of supplication. 'I've known Nessa for years, Luc. I know her whole family. They've been riding horses since before they could walk. Her sister and father are excellent trainers. I've seen Nessa race—she's not done many, granted, but she's got her licence and she's a natural. We were short a rider today and so I asked Mrs Owens if I could borrow her. I don't know what she's doing working for your housekeeper, Luc, but she's wasted there. She should be out here. All she's been waiting for is an opportunity to prove herself.'

If it had been anyone else but his trusted and very talented trainer, and if Luc hadn't seen her with his own two eyes, he would have fired Pete on the spot. And he wasn't about to tell Pete why Nessa was working at the house.

He looked back at the gallops to see the riders dismounting and walking the horses back to the stables. He spotted her immediately, the smallest of the bunch, immediately bringing to mind how tight she'd felt when he'd breached her body. *Virgin. No protection.* And he still wanted her with a hunger that unnnerved him.

Oblivious to what was going on in his head, Pete said, 'Luc, I think you should use her in the next race. Give her a chance.'

Luc looked at Pete, provocation and frustration boiling over. 'You've done enough for now. I don't care how talented a jockey she is, she knew better than to say yes to your request.'

Nessa was still buzzing with adrenalin after exercising the horse, and chatting with the other riders, some of whom she knew. They'd all been curious as to why she was here but she'd kept it vague.

She was in the changing room and had just pulled off her mud-spattered top when the door slammed open and she whirled around, holding the shirt to her chest. 'Do you mind?'

But it wasn't Pete or one of the other riders entering the ladies' changing room near the racing stables. It was Luc Barbier and he looked murderous. The door shut behind him with an ominously quiet click, and the room was suddenly tiny.

She'd deliberately avoided thinking about Luc's reaction if he found out. Apparently for good reason.

He stood before the door in worn jeans and a black polo shirt. He'd never looked more forbiddingly sexy. Nessa's insides melted even as she tried to ignore her body's response. Luc hadn't come near her for the past couple of days, making it perfectly clear that the other night couldn't have been a bigger mistake. And while Nessa agreed on every rational level, she hated to admit that she'd been hurt by the dismissal.

Guilt lanced her now. Had she agreed to Pete's request to fill in for one of the jockeys, knowing Luc wouldn't approve, to provoke a reaction? Nessa was afraid she knew the answer to that.

'What the hell do you think you're doing?' Luc's voice was quiet, which made him sound even angrier.

Nessa lifted her chin, refusing to be intimidated, clutching her top to her chest. 'Pete was short a rider and so he asked me if I'd fill in. I was just doing him a favour.' *Liar*, mocked a voice. The thrumming of her pulse told her very eloquently why she'd done it.

'You knew very well that you weren't allowed to go near the horses. I don't let anyone that I don't personally vet myself near them.'

Nessa tried not to sound defensive. 'Pete knows me. He's seen me ride before. And it wasn't his fault,' she said hurriedly, having visions of Luc sacking him. 'I knew I should have said no…but I couldn't resist. It's my fault.'

Once again Luc was struck somewhere uncomfortable at how readily Nessa was able to take the blame from someone else. Her brother, and now Pete, who wasn't even related to her.

As if physically incapable of allowing space between them, Luc moved closer, seeing how Nessa's hands tightened on her top. He commented, 'It's not as if I haven't seen you before.'

She blushed. Amazingly. And it had a direct effect on Luc's body, sending blood surging south.

She scooted her head and arms back into her top but not before Luc had seen a generous amount of pale flesh and her breasts encased in a sports vest top. Her hair was caught at the back of her head in a bun, and he curled his hands to fists to stop from reaching out and undoing it.

She folded her arms over her chest and then said stiffly, 'I'm sorry. It won't happen again.'

Luc made a split-second decision. 'I'm afraid that's not really up to you.'

She looked at him. 'What do you mean?'

'There's a race this weekend; I want you to ride the same filly you were just riding.'

She went pale, and then colour washed back into her cheeks. It was fascinating to see someone so expressive. And then she looked suspicious. 'You don't want me near your horses. Why would you let me do this?'

'Because I'm not stupid enough to let someone as naturally gifted as you waste your talent, especially not when it might win me a race. I am, after all, running a business. And your brother owes me a million euros, which you have taken on as your debt. If you win, the money will go towards paying it off.'

Nessa was so stunned by what he'd just proposed she was speechless for a long moment. Eventually she managed to get out, 'I...well, thank you.'

Luc was brusque. 'You'll obviously work to Pete's instruction from now on.'

Then he turned to walk back out and Nessa blurted out, 'Wait.'

When he stopped at the door he turned around and she almost lost her nerve, but she forced herself to ask, 'What about what happened? The other night.' *As if he wouldn't know what she was talking about.*

She cringed inwardly. She hated that she'd felt compelled to ask. She hated that she couldn't be as nonchalant as him, and pretend the other night had never happened.

Luc looked remote. Almost like a stranger. 'What happened between us won't happen again. It was a mistake. You're here to pay off the debt through racing or until your brother returns my money, whichever happens first.'

And then he walked out and she felt as if he'd just punched her in the belly. She was breathless, and then she castigated herself. Hadn't he warned her, that first night in his room, that she'd get burned?

She had nothing to entice a man like Luc Barbier beyond that brief moment of craziness.

And here he was offering her the opportunity of a lifetime—a chance to ride for one of the great trainer/ owners in the racing world. Luc might have a rogue's reputation but no one could discredit his amazing accomplishments, even if they weren't quite sure how he'd achieved them without a background steeped in the industry.

Nessa had to concede that, from what she'd seen so far, his incredible work ethic was responsible for much of his success. Without fail, he was up with his earliest employee, and probably one of the last to bed. She'd even seen him help with mucking out a stables one day, practically unheard of for someone at his level.

Nessa told herself she should be relieved that Luc had laid out in brutal terms where they now stood in terms of their short-lived intimacy. Conducting an affair with a man like him was total folly at best and emotional suicide at worst. Not to mention the guilt she'd feel.

But the most humiliating part of it was knowing that if he'd kissed her just now, she'd have been flat on her back on the cold tile floor, showing not an ounce of restraint or control.

* * *

'I can't believe she's actually won.'

'Never fail to surprise us, eh, Barbier?'

'A female jockey? Who is she? Has anyone heard of her? Where did she come from?'

'Trust Barbier to come from left-field with a win like this...he just can't resist throwing the cat amongst the pigeons...'

Luc heard all the indiscreet whispers around him, but he was too stunned to care. Nessa had won the race. Unbelievably. On the horse with the longest odds.

She was coming into the winner's enclosure now, with Pete not far behind accepting his own congratulations. Luc caught the horse as she passed, stopping her momentarily. Nessa had a huge grin on her mud-spattered face and something turned over inside him.

He patted the horse and looked up at her, at an uncharacteristic loss for words. Her smile faded and he noticed how she tensed and something inside him rejected that. Normally he never had a problem congratulating his jockeys but this was different. It was *her*. Eventually he said, 'Well done.'

'Thank you. I can't believe it myself.'

That glimmer of uncertainty on her face reminded him of how she'd looked the other night when she'd stood before him all mussed and flushed after sex. His body tightened with need.

She was led on, and then slid off the horse to be

weighed after the race. Luc watched her across the enclosure. She took off her hat and her hair tumbled down. A man behind him made an appreciative whistling sound and Luc spun around, glaring at him. The man blanched.

When Luc looked back Nessa was walking away from the podium and stewards with her saddle, presumably to go back to the changing rooms.

Pascal Blanc hurried over to him at that moment, shaking his head and smiling. 'Luc, this is incredible. Nessa is a sensation; it's all people are talking about, wondering who she is and where she came from. You've both been invited to a function this evening in Dublin, celebrating the racing industry in Ireland. I don't think I need to tell you how important this is.'

Luc knew exactly how important it was. So far the industry here had largely been closed to him socially, but one win with an outsider filly and a beautiful young female jockey and suddenly he was being granted access.

Yes, said a voice. *This is it*. And yet now that the moment had arrived, all Luc could seem to think about was not the potential for acceptance at last, but what Nessa would look like in a dress.

'Is it really necessary for me to attend?' Nessa's gut was churning.

'Yes, it is,' Luc said, looking frustrated. They'd returned to the racing stables after the race and Luc had just informed Nessa about the function in Dublin that night.

She couldn't even begin to describe the trepidation she felt at the thought of some glitzy social event. She'd never been a naturally girly girl and her few experiences of dressing up had invariably ended in failure when she'd seen how wide of the mark she was with current trends.

There'd been one memorable incident in university when she'd gone to a party and a girl had said snarkily, *I didn't know it was a fancy dress party.* After that, Nessa had given up trying to fit in. She wasn't cool, or fashionable, or blessed with any innate feminine wiles or sensuality. Luc had proved that in no uncertain terms.

'I don't have anything suitable to wear to an event.'

Luc glanced at his watch. 'I've asked a stylist to come from a local boutique with a selection of dresses. She's also bringing someone to look after hair and make-up.'

Nessa felt as if a noose were tightening around her neck. Luc was still dressed in a three-piece suit, in deference to the dress etiquette of the races. It was distracting to say the least, especially in the way that it seemed to be moulded to his muscles.

'Why is it so important that I go? I'm just the jockey. They won't know who I am.'

Luc took out his mobile phone and, after a few seconds of swiping, handed it to Nessa. She gasped. It was a headline on an online racing journal. *Two gorgeous fillies triumph at the Kilkenny Gold Stakes!* And there was a photo of a beaming Nessa astride the horse, being led around the winner's enclosure.

'Unfortunate headlines aside, you're a sensation. Everyone could see, just from that race, how talented you are.'

Nessa handed the phone back, feeling a little sick. She'd wanted to do well, but she'd never expected this level of attention. The euphoria of the win was draining away to be replaced with anxiety. She'd never liked being front and centre, and certainly not in an environment outside her comfort zone.

Her sister Iseult had struggled with this kind of thing too, but she'd since blossomed into a poised and elegent Sheikha of Merkazad. Even so, she had confessed to Nessa that she still found it hard sometimes to pretend that she was comfortable with dressing up.

But Nadim loved her no matter how she looked or what she wore. A pang lanced Nessa to think of their bond. She felt very alone all of a sudden.

'What's wrong?'

Luc's question jolted Nessa out of her reverie. He was frowning down at her, and she hated the thought of him seeing an ounce of the vulnerability she felt. She was being ridiculous. It was just an event.

She tipped up her chin. 'Nothing is wrong. What time should I meet the stylist?'

'They'll be here within the hour. I've asked Mrs Owens to move you to a bigger bedroom suite to accommodate you getting ready. We may have more events like this to go to. I'll meet you at the front of the house at seven p.m.'

Nessa looked at herself in the mirror and blinked. *Was that her?* She felt the same inside, but on the outside she looked like a stranger. Her hair was pulled back on one side and trailed over her other shoulder in a rippling cascade of glossy waves. She wore a shimmering black dress that clung to her shoulders in a wide vee, and showed what felt like acres of pale flesh.

It was gathered under her breasts and fell in a swathe of material to the floor. Under the dress she wore spindly delicate high heels that made her walk with her chest out and with an unnatural arch in her back.

Her make-up was discreet, at least, but it made her eyes look huge. Her lips glistened with flesh-coloured lipstick.

The stylist stood back and looked at her critically. 'You look stunning, Miss O'Sullivan.'

'Call me Nessa, please,' Nessa said weakly, feeling like a fraud.

The stylist looked at her watch as the hair and make-up girl tidied up her things.

'It's almost seven p.m. You should go down to meet Mr Barbier.' The stylist winked. 'What I wouldn't give to swap places with you right now. He is *gorgeous*.'

The make-up girl giggled, clearly of the same opinion. Nessa forced a smile and desisted from saying that she'd be more than happy to swap places. But they wouldn't understand.

She made her way downstairs, careful in the high-heels. When she got to the hallway the door was ajar and she went out. Luc was standing with his back to her on the steps, his hands in his pockets, the jacket material pulled taut across his back. It reminded her of the scar she'd seen and how he'd dismissed it so enigmatically.

For the brief moment before he turned around Nessa could almost imagine she was one of those beautiful women who populated his world, and that this was a date. But then he turned around, and those dark eyes raked her from head to toe without an ounce of emotion or expression on his face and Nessa didn't feel beautiful any more. She was remembering how he'd told her that first night that even if she'd come via the front door and dressed to impress, she still wouldn't be his type...

For a second Luc almost didn't recognise Nessa. His chest tightened and his whole body went taut with the need to control his instantaneous response.

She looked beautiful. She surpassed anything he could have possibly imagined, and yet there was nothing showy about her. She oozed understated elegance in the long black dress. His body lit on fire when he registered the low-cut vee and saw how much of her skin was exposed, including the pale swells of her breasts.

He dragged his gaze back up, feeling a little dizzy. He saw her biting her lip, and looking anxious. 'Is it okay?' she asked.

Luc was a little incredulous. Did she really have no idea how gorgeous she was? His reaction to her, and his instincts urging him to believe this wasn't an act, made his voice curt. 'It's fine. We should go.'

Nessa tried not to feel disappointed by Luc's reaction as he turned away and went down the steps, towards where a sleek four-wheeled drive was parked. The other night was a mistake, not to be repeated, and this was *not* a date.

She made her way across the courtyard after him in the vertiginous heels, praying she wouldn't sprain her ankle. He was holding a door open and she got in gingerly, holding the dress up so it wouldn't get caught.

Luc walked around the bonnet. Nessa couldn't help observing how good he looked in the tuxedo. When he was behind the wheel he drove them a few short miles to where a helipad was located, away from the racing stables and stud.

'We're going in a helicopter?'

He looked at her. 'It's an hour's drive to Dublin. The event starts in half an hour.'

Nessa tried her best to look nonchalant and not shocked. When she stepped out of the car, though, she stopped. The grass was soft and damp after recent rain and she wasn't sure how to navigate the terrain in her shoes from here to where the helicopter was waiting.

Luc came around the front of the car and saw her, obviously assessing her predicament. Nessa was about to bend down and take the shoes off, but before she could do so Luc had lifted her into his arms effortlessly and was striding towards the helicopter where a pilot was waiting by the open door.

Nessa clung to his neck breathlessly, burningly aware of his hard chest and strong arms. Luc however showed no such similar awareness when he deposited her into the seat with a grim expression and did up her seat belt before she could object. His hands glanced off her bare skin as he adjusted it and Nessa's blood fizzed.

She was glad when he sat in the front beside the pilot because she didn't want him to decipher what she was thinking. He couldn't have made it more glaringly obvious that she was just someone he was tolerating, until such a time as she ceased to be a thorn in his side.

When they'd put on their headphones he turned around. 'Okay?'

She nodded rapidly and forced a bright smile wanting to leave him under no illusion that she was anything other than *okay* and completely unmoved by what had happened between them.

They took off and, as much as she hated Luc Bar-

bier right now, she couldn't help feeling emotional
when they swooped low over the River Liffey in
Dublin's city centre and she saw the capital city glittering like a jewel in the dusky evening light. It was
magical.

They landed, and Nessa was saved the ignominy
of being carried again as she was able to walk to the
car waiting for them. Luc sat in the back with her,
and the plush interior, which looked huge, felt tiny
with him so close to her.

The journey to Dublin Castle took ten minutes
and soon they were pulling up in the majestic fore-
court. Lights shone out onto the cobbles as a glittering array of people were disgorged from sleek cars.
And Nessa—who had just won her first prestigious
race on a thoroughbred horse—had never felt more
terrified in her life.

Luc got out and came around to help Nessa out. She
looked at his hand for a moment, hesitating, and then
took it, letting him help her. As soon as she was
standing, though, she let go as if burned.

Luc figured that he couldn't blame her after his
less than gracious reaction to how she looked. He'd
never been less charming. With other women he
at least put on a show of being civilised. But with
Nessa, he didn't know where to put himself.

When he'd picked her up to carry her over the
grass to the helicopter it had been purely for expedi-
ency, but it had been torture to feel her slender frame

curling into his, her arms around his neck. He'd been as hard as a rock for the entire journey.

It irritated the hell out of him that he'd made it more than clear that what had happened between them was a one-off mistake, and she didn't seem in the least inclined to try and change his mind.

Mind you, in a dress like the one she was wearing, she didn't have to do much. He was already aware of men around them looking at her twice. He was also aware of the way he felt inclined to bundle her back into the car, and take her straight to some private place where he could lay her out on a bed and make love to her as he *hadn't* done the first time.

Her first time. Surely, whispered a wicked little voice, *she deserves to know what it can really be like?*

Luc shut it down and put out his arm for Nessa to take. He had the feeling when she slipped her arm through his that she was only touching him to stay upright in those vertiginous heels. They added inches to her height and only made him more aware of how much closer her mouth would be to his.

Then he noticed how pale she was. He stopped just before they walked into the pool of golden light spilling out onto the beautiful enclosed courtyard of the castle. 'Is something wrong?'

She shook her head and glanced at him briefly, shooting him a fake smile. 'Everything is fine. Why wouldn't it be?'

'Because you look like you're about to walk the

plank rather than walk amongst your peers at one of
the highest profile society events of the year.'

She made an inelegant snorting sound. 'Peers?
Don't make me laugh.'

Luc was shocked at the bitter tone to her voice.
He'd never heard it before. But before he could ask
her what she meant, a young officious woman in a
long violet gown was coming forward to greet them.
She was the PR lady. 'Mr Barbier, Miss O'Sullivan,
we're so grateful you could both join us at short notice. Please, do come this way.'

They were led through the marbled foyer into a
huge ceremonial room where the drinks reception
was being held before the dinner. Luc noticed people
turning to look, and how their eyes widened when
they saw who it was. He usually would have wanted
to snarl at them that he had as much of a right to be
here as they did. But for the first time, he found himself not really caring how they were looking at him.

He was too distracted by the woman by his side.

They were served with champagne and Nessa
took her arm out of Luc's. Perversely he wanted
to take it back. She was looking up at him with a
minute smile playing around her mouth. He said,
'What?'

'You said I looked as if I was about to walk the
plank but you look as if you're about to take someone's head off.'

Luc relaxed his features, unnerved she'd read him
so well.

'Haven't you been to this event before?' she asked.

Luc took a healthy swig of champagne and shook his head. 'No. They've never deigned to invite me. I was too much on the edges of acceptability for them.'

'So you don't want to be here?'

Luc looked out over the crowd and noted the furtive glances he drew. 'Whether or not I want to be here is beside the point. I've worked as hard as anyone here, harder, perhaps. I deserve to be respected and not stared at like an exhibit in a zoo. I deserve to be here.'

As soon as he'd spoken, he was shocked he'd let the words spill out. In a bid to divert Nessa away from asking more questions, he turned to her. 'What was that outside…? You made a comment.'

She flushed and took a sip of her own drink. Luc noted that her hands were tiny, with short, functional nails and clear varnish, unlike the elaborate claws many women sported. He also noticed that her hands looked softer already. His body thrummed with an arousal he was barely able to keep in check, especially when his taller vantage point gave him an all too enticing view of her cleavage.

'I didn't mean anything by it.'

Luc's gaze narrowed on her. 'Nessa…'

She rolled her eyes. 'I don't count these people as my peers, not really.'

'Why? You come from the same world. You have a family lineage in racing to rival any one of these guests.'

'Perhaps. But that counts for nothing when you're losing it all. When my father got ill and the stud started to go downhill, most of these people turned their backs on us, as if we were cursed. See that man over there?'

Luc followed her eyeline to a portly man with a face flushed from drink. The man caught Nessa's eye and went even redder, sidling out of sight like a crab disappearing under a rock.

'Who is he?' Luc asked.

'He's P J Connolly. Used to be one of my father's oldest friends. They grew up together. He runs the state-owned stud. He was in a position to help us out but he never did. It was only when Nadim bought us out and the farm started to recover that we became personae gratae again.'

Luc was stunned. He hadn't expected to feel any sort of affinity with Nessa. He'd assumed she'd be air-kissing old friends and acquaintances within minutes, but she too knew how the cold sting of rejection felt.

She turned back to him then and looked up. 'How *do* you know so much about horses? I can't believe it was just through your work with Leo Fouret.'

Luc balked at her question. Most people were usually too intent on believing one of the many rumours about him to ask him such a question directly.

'Didn't you hear?' he said with a lightness he didn't feel. 'I'm descended from gypsies.'

Nessa just looked at him and cocked her head to one side as if considering it. 'I don't think so.'

A weight lodged in Luc's chest at her easy dismissal of such a lurid claim. At that moment the PR lady came back to them, smiling widely. 'Mr Barbier, Miss O'Sullivan, there are a few people who would love to congratulate you on your win today. Please follow me.'

The weight in Luc's chest didn't abate as the woman led them further into the room. No one had ever looked at him as Nessa just had, without any guile or expectation for a salacious story.

CHAPTER SEVEN

NESSA WAS STILL irritated by the interruption earlier. Luc had looked as if she'd delivered an electric shock rather than asked an innocuous question. She was also still mulling over how he'd been deliberately ostracised from this milieu, and how it had obviously affected him.

They had just finished the sumptuous dinner when Nessa snuck a glance to where Luc was seated opposite her. He was talking to an older woman on his right-hand side, and as Nessa looked at him his eyes met hers and a shaft of sensation went straight into her gut.

She quickly looked away and put her napkin to her mouth, almost knocking over her glass in the process, in a bid to disguise that she'd been staring. When she could risk another glance, she saw the tiniest smile playing around the corners of his mouth, and it couldn't have been due to what the woman was saying because she looked all too serious.

Damn him. Nessa wanted to kick him. He must

know exactly what his effect on her was—he'd been the one to awaken her, after all. She felt intensely vulnerable and averted her eyes from then on. Then the chairman got up to make a speech, so thankfully she could focus on that and not Luc. She tuned most of it out except the bit where he said, '…and we'd like to say welcome to our newest import, all the way from France. Luc Barbier stunned the crowds today with a spectacular win…'

Nessa looked at Luc and saw him incline his head in acknowledgement of the chairman's gushing praise. The expression on his face was cool, not for a second revealing anything. Nessa wondered what he was thinking. She was surprised at the affront she felt on his behalf that he hadn't ever been invited before now.

Then she got a mention too and her face flamed bright red as everyone in the room turned their attention to her.

When the speech was over the guests got up to go to a different room where soft jazz was playing. Nessa felt awkward standing alone, not sure if Luc was going to leave her to her own devices now that everyone was lining up to speak to him. She longed to take off the shoes, which were killing her, but to her surprise Luc came straight around the table and walked up to her.

'So, what was making you look so angry during the chairman's speech?'

Nessa blanched. She was far too expressive for her

own good, useless at hiding anything. The thought of him noticing her reaction was beyond exposing. Luc wasn't budging, waiting for her reply.

She blurted out, 'Well, it's not as if you're *new* to the scene here, is it? You've been here for a couple of years, had plenty of horses in races and won more than your fair share, not to mention your accomplishments in France.'

Luc's tone was dry. 'This community is a tight-knit one. They don't allow entry purely by dint of your owning a stud and racing stables.'

'That's ridiculous. You have as much right to be here as anyone. You have a brilliant reputation. Paddy—' She stopped abruptly and bit her lip.

Luc arched a brow. 'Paddy *what*?'

She cursed her loose tongue. 'Well, you probably won't believe me, but Paddy idolises you. You're all he talked about for the first few months he was working for you. To be honest I think part of the reason he's in hiding is because he's so mortified that he let you down…'

Luc looked at Nessa. He knew vaguely that he should be working the room, capitalising on being welcomed into the fold, but he was more intrigued by this conversation. Disturbingly he did seem to recall Paddy Jnr's rather puppy-like manner and the way he'd followed Luc around for the first few weeks. When Paddy had first disappeared Luc had recalled his slavish devotion and had seen it in a more suspicious light. But now…

Nessa went on. 'He thinks you're a maverick, and he admired your unorthodox methods.'

Luc battled with the urge to trust what Nessa was saying. 'You say one thing but his actions say something else. They're nice words, Nessa, but I don't need staff idolising me. I just need people I can trust.'

'Who *do* you trust?'

'Almost no one,' Luc answered and for the first time in his life it didn't feel like something to be proud of. Disgruntled at the turn in conversation, and not liking how Nessa's affront on his behalf made him feel, he took her arm and led her into the other room where couples were already dancing.

But as soon as they approached the dance floor she became a dead weight under his hand. He glanced at her and she was pale and had a terror-struck expression on her face. Something sharp lanced him in his chest. 'What's wrong?'

She shook her head. 'I can't dance.'

'Everyone can dance. Even me.' He hadn't actually intended on dancing but now he was intrigued.

She started to pull away. 'No, really, I'll just watch. There have to be any number of women here who'd love to dance with you.'

Luc couldn't say he was unaware of the fact that a few women seemed to be circling, but apparently he was with the only woman in the room who *didn't* want to be with him. It was a novelty he didn't welcome.

He moved his hand down her arm to her hand and gripped it firmly and tugged her very reluctant body onto the dance floor.

Nessa felt sick. This was her worst nightmare. She hated dancing in public with a passion and could already hear the laughs and jeers of her brothers ringing in her ears. *Come on, Ness, you can't actually trip over your own feet—oops, she just did!*

'Really, I would rather just—' But her words dried up in her throat when Luc pulled her into his chest and put an arm around her back, then took her hand in his, holding it close to his chest.

Suddenly they were moving, and Nessa had no idea how her feet were even capable of such a thing, but suddenly she was being propelled backwards. No one was staring. Well, they were, but it was at Luc, not her.

Her tension eased slightly but then she became aware of how it felt to be so close to his body. Her eyeline was somewhere around his throat. She was still a full foot smaller than him, even in heels, and she felt very conscious of the taller and more swan-like women that glided past with their partners.

The more she thought about it, the more she had to wonder if she'd hallucinated what had happened in the stables. Right now, aside from her own thundering heart-rate and physical awareness of him, Luc could have been a total, polite stranger.

And then he looked down at her and said, 'I never

really congratulated you on your win today. If you perform like that again, you could be the face of a new generation of women jockeys.'

Had that been today? It felt like years ago. Nessa blushed, not expecting praise from this man. 'It could have been a fluke. If I do badly at the next race it won't help your reputation, or my career.'

Luc shook his head. 'You handled her beautifully. Where did you learn to ride like that?'

Nessa swallowed. The air suddenly felt thicker. She looked at Luc's bow tie. That seemed safer than looking up into the dark eyes that made her feel as if she were drowning.

'My father, before he got too ill. But mainly Iseult; she's got the real talent. I was never off a horse really, as soon as I got home from school and then every weekend when I came home from university—'

'You went to university?'

Nessa looked up. 'Iseult insisted we all go. She knew I wanted to be a jockey and she helped me, but she made sure I had something else to fall back on. The world of racing for female jockeys isn't exactly…easy.'

'What did you study?'

'Business and economics.'

Luc arched a brow. 'That's a little removed from racing.'

Nessa felt self-conscious. 'I know, and it kept me off the scene for a few years. But I didn't mind, really. I wanted to learn how to take care of our business if anything happened again.'

'Even though your brother-in-law is a sheikh and rich as Croesus?'

Nessa gave him a withering look. 'None of us expect handouts from Nadim. Not even my sister, and she's married to him! And anyway, Iseult hadn't met Nadim by the time I began university, so things were still pretty grim. I knew I didn't have the luxury of doing what I wanted and following a precarious career path.'

Luc had to admit to a grudging respect for Nessa and what her family had obviously been through. Unless of course it was all lies designed to impress him. But as much as he hated to admit it, he didn't think it was.

Since he'd discovered she was a virgin and wasn't putting on some innocent act, it had shifted his perception whether he liked it or not. Also, he could verify her story pretty easily if he looked into it.

She looked up at him again and he saw something like determination in her eyes. 'You never did answer my question earlier…how you came to know so much about horses.'

Luc cursed the fact that they were so close and surrounded by couples. No escape. But then, what did he have to hide except a very banal answer?

'An old man lived in the apartment next to my mother's. He paid me sometimes to do odd-jobs for him, shopping, things like that. He used to be a champion jockey as a young man but an accident had ruined his career. I was always fascinated by his stories and the fact that every thoroughbred today is descended—'

'From just three Arab stallions,' Nessa finished. 'I know, that's always fasincated me too.'

'Pierre became a chronic online gambler but in spite of knowing everything about every single horse's lineage and form he always lost more than he won. He taught me almost everything, including how to invest prudently, which was ironic because he never took his own advice.'

Nessa felt ridiculously emotional to think of a young Luc Barbier spending all that time with an old injured jockey. 'He sounds like an amazing person. Is he still alive?'

Luc suddenly looked more remote. He shook his head. 'He died when I was a teenager. Before he died, though, he gave me Leo Fouret's number and told me I should call him and impress him with my knowledge of racing, and that if I did he might take me on.'

Which he obviously had. Nessa was a little stunned. But before she could ask Luc any more questions she felt him pull her in much closer to avoid colliding with another couple. She'd almost forgotten they were on a dance floor, surrounded by people.

And then she felt it. The press of his body against her lower abdomen. His arousal.

She looked up, eyes wide, cheeks flaring with heat. Luc arched a brow in silent question as they kept moving, which only exacerbated the situation.

Nessa could hardly breathe. The previous conversation and revelations were forgotten. All she could think about now was the way he'd been so cold the other day in the changing rooms. *What happened between us won't happen again.*

She'd thought he'd meant he no longer desired her. 'I thought you said it wouldn't happen again.' Nessa had just assumed that her virginal state was a huge turn-off.

'I meant what I said,' Luc answered now.

Nessa was confused, and aroused. 'But…' She couldn't articulate it.

'But I still want you?'

She nodded dumbly, feeling completely out of her depth and clueless as to how to handle this situation.

Something stark crossed Luc's face. 'Just because I want you doesn't mean I have to act on it. I don't have relationships with staff.'

Nessa wanted to point out she was hardly staff, as she was working for free, but she was afraid it would sound pleading.

It was torture to be this close to him, knowing that he did want her but could act so cool about it. She was not cool. She was the opposite of cool. Her insides were going on fire and between her legs was hot and slippery.

Emotion was rising and bubbling over before she could stop it. She felt especially vulnerable after hearing his story about the old jockey. She pulled free of his embrace. 'You said you don't play games but maybe you lied, Luc. I think you're toying with me as a form of punishment. You know you're more experienced than me so maybe this is how you get your kicks.'

Nessa walked quickly off the dance floor—as quickly as she could in the heels. To her horror, she felt tears prick the backs of her eyes and she was almost running by the time she reached the foyer.

A man stepped forward. 'Miss O'Sullivan?'

It took her a second to recognise the driver. And then his eyes lifted to something, or someone, behind her. *Luc.* Nessa composed herself, aghast that she'd run like that. The last thing she wanted was for him to know he affected her emotionally.

The driver melted away again and Nessa turned around reluctantly. Luc caught her arm and tugged her over to a discreet corner. He was grim. 'I told you before that I don't play games. And I don't get off by denying myself, believe me—this is new territory for me.'

Nessa felt slightly mollified by that. Maybe she'd overreacted. And now she was embarrassed. If anything she should be rejoicing that he wasn't taking advantage of her lack of control around him.

She pulled her arm free, avoiding Luc's eye. 'It's late, and I promised Pete I'd be up early to train for the next race tomorrow.'

Eventually Luc just said, 'I'll have Brian drive you home. I have a meeting to attend tomorrow morning here in town so I'll stay the night.'

Nessa hated herself for the betraying lurch she felt, as if she'd been hoping that Luc might have said something else, like *stay*. She stepped back. 'Goodnight, Luc.'

He called Brian on his mobile phone and the driver reappeared. Within seconds of Luc delivering his instructions Nessa was in the back of the car, being driven swiftly away from Dublin Castle and back out to Luc's racing stables.

She cringed with humiliation the whole way because, whether he'd intended it or not, Luc had just proven that he might still want her, but she was the last woman on earth he'd take into his bed again. She might've felt like Cinderella going to the ball tonight, but wearing a pretty dress and dancing with a prince wasn't enough to make her a princess.

A short time later, Luc stood with a towel slung around his waist on the balcony of his opulent hotel suite. The moon reflected off the River Liffey where it snaked its way through Dublin city centre. He could hear late night revellers' shouts drifting up from the street. He took a sip of the finest Irish whiskey, but nothing could put a dent in the levels of his arousal. Not even the cold shower he'd just taken.

What the hell was he thinking denying himself the pleasures of female flesh? Even if it was Nessa O'Sullivan and she came with a million and one complications.

Because of the way she looks at you...and because of the questions she asks that reach right down to a place you don't care to analyse.

Luc cursed. He'd told her about Pierre. Pierre Fortin had been one of Luc's saving graces while growing up, teaching him about this fantastical world of horses and racing.

Luc had called his very first racehorse Fortin's Legacy, after his friend.

He never spoke about Pierre. It was too personal, too close to the bone. Sometimes grief for his old friend resurfaced, taking him by surprise with its intensity. But, for the first time, he felt as if he'd done a disservice to his friend by not talking about him more.

Luc cursed again. Tricky questions or no tricky questions, he still wanted Nessa. He realised now that denying himself the carnal satisfaction of taking her to bed again was doing nothing but messing with his head.

He wanted her on a physical level. That was all. And maybe if he reminded her of the physical, it would dissuade her from thinking about anything else. Like asking awkward questions that he wasn't interested in answering or thinking about.

Nessa came second in the next race. Not a win but very respectable all the same. Pete was ecstatic. As for Luc—his reaction, Nessa couldn't figure out, because his expression was always so unreadable and he'd given nothing away when she'd seen him on the sidelines after she'd finished the race.

A few days had passed since the function and she'd hardly seen him. Apparently he'd been in Dublin for meetings, and he'd also visited Paris in the meantime.

Nessa told herself that she didn't care, as she checked herself in the mirror of the VIP guests' bathroom. She pulled at the cream lace pencil skirt she was wearing, feeling overdressed. It had a matching top. Pascal had told her she'd need to dress up for the press, so she'd brought some of the clothes that the stylist had left for her from the night of the function.

She'd pulled her hair back so it looked as sleek as possible and had it in a low bun at the back of her head, and she wore one of those ridiculous-looking fascinator hats, set to the side of her head. She sighed, hoping she looked presentable, and made her way to the VIP room to meet Pascal.

When she got to the plush suite, however, it was empty. There were some refreshments lined up on a table but Nessa ignored her growling stomach and helped herself to some water, not wanting to be caught with a bun in her mouth and crumbs all over her clothes.

The room had an enviable view of the track where races were still being run, but it was blocked off from the other suites, making it very private.

She heard the door open behind her and turned

around to greet Pascal and whatever press he'd
brought with him but it wasn't Pascal. It was Luc,
in his three-piece suit. Looking like the most uncivilised civilised man on the planet.

His dark gaze swept up and down and Nessa's
skin prickled with self-consciousness and awareness.
'Pascal told me to dress appropriately for the press.'

'You look very...*appropriate*,' Luc said. Nessa
heard the unmistakable turning of the lock in the
door, and her heart-rate increased as Luc prowled
into the room like a predator approaching his prey.

Nessa took a step back and said nervously, 'Pascal and the press are going to be here any minute.'

Luc shook his head. 'He's keeping them busy else-
where for a little while.'

Nessa felt confused. 'Why did you lock us in here?'

Now he was in front of her and looked very tall.
And fierce, and sexy. Her body was reacting in spite
of her best intentions to try and remain immune to
his appeal.

'I locked us in here because I'm done denying
myself where you're concerned.'

Luc put his hand around the back of her head, and
before she knew what was happening she could feel
her carefully constructed bun being undone and her
hair was falling down her back. The silly, frivolous
hat ended up on the floor.

'Luc, what are you doing?' Why did she sound
so breathy?

In a silent answer, he pulled her into his body,

tipped her face up and kissed her. Nessa had no defence for this sensual ambush. Her whole body ignited as if it had just been waiting for his kiss and touch.

Luc was like a marauding warrior, leaving no space to think about what was happening. All she could do was *feel*. Succumb. She'd wanted to experience this again so much, and now that it was happening she never wanted it to stop.

Before she could control herself her arms were lifting to wrap around his neck and she was arching her body into his, straining to get closer. His hands moved up and down her back, tracing her waist, going under her top to find the bare skin between that and her skirt.

But, like a cool wind skating over her skin, reality intruded, and she mustered up every ounce of strength she had to pull free.

Nessa was breathing as if she'd just run a marathon. Luc's eyes were burning and she belatedly noticed the stubble on his jaw. She could feel the burn on her skin like a mocking brand.

'What's wrong?'

'What's wrong?' Nessa wrapped her arms around herself defensively. 'You said this wouldn't happen again.'

His face was stark. 'I thought I could resist you, Nessa…but I can't. This will burn up, but then it'll fizzle out. It always does. Let me be the one to teach you how it can be, for as long as we want each other.'

She shivered inside. He'd already done a pretty good job of teaching her how it could be. There was something very illicitly enticing about the prospect of burning up with this man and then letting it *fizzle out*. But she had to be strong. She shook her head. 'I don't think this is a good idea.'

His jaw tightened. She spoke again before he could. 'I'm not just some convenient plaything you can discard and pick up again when it suits you.'

'Believe me,' he growled, 'there's nothing convenient about how I feel about this, or you.'

Nessa smarted. 'Well, I'm sure there are plenty of women who would be far more *convenient* than me.'

He shook his head and closed the distance between them, reaching out to cup her jaw, a thumb moving against her skin hypnotically.

'The problem is that I don't want any other woman. I only want *you*.'

Nessa's throat went dry. Luc Barbier telling her he wanted only her was more than she could handle. Treacherously, she could feel her resistance weaken.

Her heart thumped unevenly. As if trying to soothe a nervy foal, Luc gently cupped her face with his hands, tipping it up to him. He filled her vision.

'I want *you*, Nessa.'

Her mind raced. Could she really handle another intimate encounter with this man? He was already sliding under her skin in a way that mocked her for thinking she could separate her emotions from the physicality.

Dark grey eyes held her captive. 'This is just physical. Don't overthink it. It has nothing to do with your brother or the debt. This is just for us.'

He was saying all the right things to make her weaken even more. *Just physical*. She could keep her emotions out of it if he could.

Nessa was afraid she could no more refuse what Luc was offering than she could stop taking her next breath. She reached up and traced the hard sensual line of his mouth with her finger, overwhelmed that he wanted her so much.

A sense of fatality filled her. She knew she couldn't resist. She reached up and pressed her mouth against his in a silent gesture of capitulation, unable to articulate it any other way.

Luc didn't like to acknowledge the surge of triumph he felt when Nessa's mouth touched his. He didn't like to think of the swirl of emotions he'd just seen in her expressive green eyes. But it wasn't enough to stop him.

He wrapped his arms around her and backed her up against the wall so that he could fully explore that lush and sexy mouth that had been haunting his dreams for days now.

She was as sweet as he remembered. Sweeter. Her small tongue darted out to touch his, and went back again. He captured it, sucking it deep, making her squirm against him. His aching flesh ground into her soft contours and Luc knew that there was no stopping this now. He had to have her with a hunger that was unprecedented.

Somehow a sliver of cold realism entered his head and he took his mouth off Nessa's for a moment. 'I need you, here, right now...'

She looked up at him, eyes molten pools of desire. Slightly glazed. She bit her lip. 'Okay.'

Luc took his hands off her even though it was the hardest thing. 'Take off your clothes.'

Nessa shivered, feeling vulnerable for a moment, but then Luc started to disrobe and she couldn't take her eyes off him as he cast aside his jacket, waistcoat, tie, shirt, and unbuckled his belt.

In a bid to try and keep breathing, Nessa reached for the zip at her neck, but her fingers fumbled and were clumsy. Luc was bare-chested, his trousers open, showing the trail of dark hair that led down into his underwear. She couldn't function.

He stepped forward and said, 'Turn around.'

She did. His hand came to her zip, pulling it down, and then the top slid off from her front. He opened her bra and turned her to face him, pulling it off completely. The crowds outside the VIP box roared as another race was won, but Nessa barely noticed.

Luc discarded his trousers and she could see where the material of his underwear was tented over his erection. Her mouth watered.

'Your skirt. Take it off, now.'

The rough quality of his voice made the flames

lick even higher. Nessa knew she should be feeling more self-conscious as she shimmied out of the skirt but she felt emboldened under Luc's appreciative gaze.

For the first time in her life she felt a very feminine thrill of power. It was heady to know she had this effect on a man like Luc Barbier, who was normally so in control.

As soon as the skirt pooled at her feet, she kicked off her shoes and dropped a few inches in height. Luc yanked down his underwear, freeing himself, and pulled her close, wrapping his arms around her and hauling her up and into him as his mouth landed on hers and he devoured her.

She loved the feel of his hard body next to hers. It made her feel delicate and soft. Her arms twined around his neck as she lost herself in his kiss and she wasn't even aware that he'd carried her over to a seat until the earth tilted and she realised he was sitting down and she was straddling his lap.

His hands felt huge on her back and his mouth was on a level with her breasts. He surrounded one hard peak in hot, wet, sucking heat and Nessa's head fell back. When his teeth teased her tender flesh she sucked in a breath, tensing all over.

His erection was thick and long between them. She reached down and touched him, feeling the bead of moisture at the tip. He hissed a breath and she heard the sound of foil being broken before Luc set her back slightly to roll protection onto his length.

He reached for her again, putting his hands on her hips. 'Sit up slightly…that's it…'

As he manoeuvred her into position over his body, Nessa had never felt more animalistic, or earthy and raw. Luc ripped the side of her panties so they were no longer an impediment, and she felt the thick, blunt head of his erection against her slippery folds.

She had a moment of remembering the brief pain of his first penetration, but as if he were reading her mind his hand soothed her, up and down her back, and he said, 'Trust me, *minou*…it won't hurt again, okay?'

She nodded, bracing her hands on his shoulders as he slowly joined their bodies. Nessa couldn't look away from his eyes as, inch by inch, he filled her so completely that she couldn't breathe.

'You dictate the pace, *ma belle*…'

Luc's voice sounded strained and Nessa felt that rush of feminine power again as she experimented by moving up and down on his body, rolling her hips.

He huffed a laugh against her breast. 'You're going to kill me…'

But Nessa was too distracted by the building tension at her core and how, by moving faster, she could make it build and build. Luc was pressing kisses all over her bared skin, his teeth and mouth teasing her breasts unmercifully. Nessa's movements became wilder, more desperate, as she sensed the shimmering peak approaching. She was losing control. But just as she thought that, Luc took over, demonstrating his experience and mastery.

He clamped his hands onto her hips, holding her still as his body pumped up into hers, stronger and harder and deeper than before.

Sweat glistened on their skin, black eyes burning into hazel. Nessa couldn't hold on. She thought she might die, and then with one cataclsymic thrust she did, but it was an exquisite death that brought with it rolling wave upon wave of pleasure. It was so intense that she had to bite his shoulder to stop herself from screaming out loud and informing the entire racetrack what was happening in this room.

In the aftermath, Nessa couldn't have said how long she was slumped against Luc's body, wrapped in his arms. Her body pulsated rythmically around his, and it sent new shivers of awareness through her.

He gently tugged her head back. She was too sated and exhausted to care how she looked.

'Next time, we make it to a bed and do this properly.'

Next time. More shivers went through her body. *This is only just beginning.*

'Next time?' She injected her voice with a lightness she didn't feel.

Luc smiled and it was wicked and sinful and gorgeous. 'Oh, yes, there'll be a next time and one after that too…and possibly even one after that.'

He punctuated his words with hot, open-mouthed

kisses along her bare shoulder. Weakly, Nessa blocked out all of the voices trying to burst the amazing afterglow bubble surrounding her and told herself that she could handle this. She could handle anything, as long as he didn't stop kissing her.

CHAPTER EIGHT

'THERE'S A HORSE at my stables in France that I'd like you to try riding. He's tricky and none of my jockeys there seem to be able to handle him.'

Nessa looked over at Luc from where she was brushing down Tempest, who she'd just been riding out on the gallops. Luc was dressed in his casual uniform of worn jeans and a long-sleeved top with boots. He leaned nonchalantly against the stable door, arms folded. He took her breath away all too easily and she had to focus to remember what he'd said. It had been two days since the X-rated interlude in the VIP suite at the track and her body still felt overly sensitised.

'Ok.'

Luc straightened up. 'When you've finished here go and pack—we'll leave in a couple of hours. We'll stay in my Paris apartment tonight for the function and go to the stables tomorrow.'

Nessa swallowed as she absorbed this information. 'The function?'

He nodded. 'We've been invited to the annual

French sports awards. Apparently you're a sensation outside of Ireland too. Everyone wants to see you up close.'

Nessa quailed at that and distracted herself by asking, 'You said we'd stay at your apartment, is that appropriate?'

Luc came towards her and he said, 'It's very appropriate. What part of *next time* didn't you understand?'

He slid his hand around the back of her neck under where her hair was gathered in a messy ponytail and tugged her towards him, saying in a low voice, 'Maybe you need reminding...'

The stable and horse were blocked out as Luc's mouth covered hers. It was so explicit that all she could think about was heat and desperate need. She was barely aware of the brush falling to the ground or the horse moving slightly, jostling them.

Luc lifted his head after a few moments and it took a second for Nessa to open her eyes. *Damn.* She was toast, as well as being well reminded.

With a smug look on his far too gorgeous face, Luc backed out of the stable and walked away, leaving Nessa standing there feeling as if a bolt of lightning had just gone through her body.

She knew that it wasn't a good idea to allow Luc to affect her like this, for many many reasons, not least of which was self-preservation. But the thought of going to Paris with him was just too seductive to resist.

* * *

A few hours later, Nessa increasingly felt as if she were in a fairy tale. She'd been to Paris before, on a school trip, but it had been nothing like this. They'd flown in by private jet and then been whisked from the airport into the centre of Paris.

Nessa had noticed that, as they'd passed the graffiti'd high walls on the motorway on the outskirts of the city, Luc had seemed to tense and had looked resolutely out of the window at something she couldn't see.

But was there a more beautiful city than Paris, with its distinctive wide boulevards and soaring magnificent buildings? Especially at this time of year, on the cusp of summer and when spring's blossoms lined the ground like a multicoloured carpet. Not to mention the iconic structures of the Arc de Triomphe and the Eiffel Tower that Nessa could see through the open doors of her bathroom right now.

When they'd arrived at Luc's apartment, at the very top of one of those massive ornate buildings on a wide boulevard, he'd disappeared into a study to take some calls, and a friendly housekeeper had shown Nessa into a guest bedroom suite.

She'd shown her a dressing room that was full to the brim of a stunning array of clothes. Nessa hadn't really known how to react to the fact that Luc was evidently always prepared for his female guests, but it had certainly been sobering. It had been just as well, she'd told herself stoutly, as she hadn't even thought to pack a dress before leaving Ireland.

Now Nessa stood in her bathrobe on the small terrace outside the French doors, and pushed everything out of her head but *this* glorious magical view. Dusk was claiming the skies and the lights of the Eiffel Tower were just beginning to twinkle to life. As if someone had been waiting especially for her.

Nessa smiled and realised with a pang that it had been a long time since she'd felt such uncomplicated happiness. The minute she thought that, though, the smile slid off her face. *How* could she be feeling happy when her brother was still probably worried sick at the thought of ever showing his face again?

She'd tried calling him earlier but his phone had been off, as it was every other time she'd tried. And her other brother, Eoin, was equally hard to track down.

Just then there was a light knock on the main bedroom door. Nessa's heart was pounding at the thought that it might be Luc, but when she opened the door, it was the housekeeper with two other women. Nessa breathed out.

'Mr Barbier has arranged for these ladies to help you get ready for this evening.'

Nessa forced a smile, the thought of the function making her feel slightly ill. Dublin was one thing. This was Paris. She would definitely need help. 'Thank you, Lucille.'

As the women set to work, Nessa tried to block

out the insidious thought of all the other women Luc had had in this exact same spot, being preened especially for him.

'Luc, it's PR gold. They love her. The fact that she's so naturally talented makes her even more interesting. There hasn't been a buzz like this about a female jockey in years. The press have also discovered her family connection to Sheikh Nadim and his wife so now there's even more heat. Invitations are flooding in—you're officially accepted into the inner sanctum now. How does it feel?'

How did it feel? The conversation he'd just had with Pascal on the phone replayed in his head, as did that question. How did it feel to finally be experiencing a measure of the acceptance and respect he'd long since craved?

Curiously anticlimactic, if Luc was brutally honest. Even this view, which took in an exclusive slice of glittering Paris, left him feeling a little hollow.

Just then he heard a noise and turned around to see Nessa in the doorway of the room. And his heart stopped. She'd been beautiful before but now she was...*stunning*.

She wore a long, shimmering green gown. She was covered up from neck to toe and it had long sleeves, but it hugged every delicate curve of her body, highlighting her lithe sensuality. Her hair was up in a chignon and she wore simple diamonds in her ears.

She walked into the room looking nervous. 'I'm ready to go.'

There was a quality to her this evening that made her seem very vulnerable. Luc could tell how out of her depth she was, and he felt a very alien need to say something to reassure her.

Far too gruffly he said, 'You look very beautiful, Nessa.'

As she blushed and smoothed the dress at her hip, he noticed the slight tremor in her hand and it tugged on something very raw inside him. This woman could ride and master a thoroughbred horse, and yet *this* made her tremble?

'I'm not beautiful. You don't have to say that.'

He closed the distance between them in two long strides and tipped up her chin, searching her eyes. 'If you were anyone else I'd say you're fishing for compliments, but I think you really mean it. Who ever made you believe that?'

She pulled her chin free. 'Growing up with two brothers makes it hard to explore your feminine side, and our mother died when I was eight, so I never really had that influence.'

'What about your older sister, Iseult?'

Nessa shrugged. 'She was a tomboy too. And she was always so busy.'

Luc tried to contain his surprise. He'd never known a beautiful woman to not make the most of her assets, until now. Nessa was all the more refreshing for it. He felt in serious danger of taking

her by the hand and leading her back to the bedroom to undo all that pristine hair and make-up. He
felt unmoored.

He stepped back. 'We should go. The driver will
be waiting for us.'

As they descended in the lift Nessa found it hard
to douse the ball of warmth Luc's words had created
in her chest. *He thought she was beautiful.* She knew
he wasn't a man to make empty compliments, and
for the first time in her life she actually felt something close to beautiful.

She took deep breaths to quell her nerves and tried
not to be too aware of Luc in the small space. But he
took up so much of it, effortlessly.

Their eyes met in the mirror of the door and any
benefits of the calm breathing Nessa had been doing
were gone in an instant. His eyes were like molten
black pools, and there was a gleam so explicit that
she couldn't breathe.

Everything tightened inside her and she wished
she knew how to react in this situation. She could
imagine that his other lovers—the ones who had also
chosen dresses from the vast array he had—would
turn to him now and twine their arms around his
neck and say something sultry and confident.

They would take control. They might even press
the Stop button and initiate an X-rated moment.
Maybe he was waiting for her to do that? Overcome
with insecurity, mixed with arousal, Nessa gabbled
the first thing that came into her head. 'It was lucky

that you're so prepared for your…er…women friends. There were a lot of dresses to choose from.'

His brows snapped into a frown at the same time as the doors opened. She stepped out and he took her arm, stopping her in her tracks. 'What's that supposed to mean?'

Nessa felt inevitable heat climb up from her chest to her face and cursed her colouring and lack of sophistication. 'The clothes in the dressing room. You obviously keep it stocked so your lovers aren't caught short.'

'Those clothes were for you. I had a stylist deliver them before we arrived. I don't entertain women at my apartment and I certainly don't keep a ready supply of clothes for them.'

Nessa was momentarily speechless. There was also a very dangerous fluttering feeling near her heart. He didn't entertain women at his apartment and yet she was here. She finally managed to get out one word. 'Oh.'

Luc looked grim, as if he'd just realised the significance of that too. He said nothing but just propelled her towards the entrance where the car and driver were waiting.

The journey to the hotel where the function was being held was taken in silence. Nessa was afraid of what else might come out of her mouth, so she kept it shut and drank in the view of Paris as they swept through the streets.

She had to remind herself that whatever overwhelming intensity she was feeling for Luc, it wasn't remotely the same for him. He was interested in her for a relatively brief moment, for some bizarre, unknown reason. If she hadn't burst into his life in such dramatic fashion out of a desire to protect her brother, there was no way she would have ever been sitting in the back of his car, dressed in a gown worth more than her annual income.

The sooner she kept reminding herself of that, the better. Because once Paddy sorted out this issue of the missing money, Nessa had no doubt she would be out of Luc Barbier's life so fast her head would be spinning.

A few hours later, Nessa was waiting for Luc in the foyer of the hotel. He was a couple of feet away, conducting a conversation with a man who had just stopped him. Nessa was glad of the brief respite. Luc had been right by her side all evening and she'd been embarrassingly aware of him, and even more acutely aware of every tiny moment he'd touched the base of her back or her arm.

Just then an accented voice said close to her ear, 'Isn't he the most beautiful thing you've ever seen?'

Nessa jumped and looked around to see an older but carefully preserved woman with blonde hair, her blue eyes fixated on Luc. There was something about the nakedly hungry gleam in her gaze that sent a shiver through Nessa.

'I'm sorry, do I know you?'

The women dragged her gaze off Luc and looked Nessa up and down disparagingly. 'You're this new jockey they're all talking about, I gather.' Her eyes narrowed. 'You're sleeping with him, aren't you?'

Nessa flushed. 'I don't think that's any of your—'

But the women grabbed her arm in an almost painful grip. She hissed at Nessa, 'He won't be tamed, you know. A magnificent beast like him will never be tamed.'

Nessa pulled her arm free and looked at the woman, feeling a hot surge of anger and something far more ambiguous. A fierce protectiveness. 'He's not an *animal*. He's a man.'

'Celeste. What a pleasure.'

Nessa's head whipped around to see Luc right behind her, looking sterner than she'd ever seen him, his glaze so black it was obsidian. Clearly it *wasn't* a pleasure.

The woman all but thrust Nessa out of the way and stepped close to Luc. 'Darling…it's been so long.' She laid a hand on his arm and a wave of revulsion went through Nessa to see the long red nails. It made her think of blood.

Luc picked off her hand and took Nessa by the arm, pulling her back beside him. 'Good evening, Celeste.'

He turned and they walked out. Nessa resisted the urge to look back at the woman. She had to be one of Luc's ex-lovers, but the thought of him with her made Nessa's stomach roil.

* * *

The car pulled away from the kerb and Luc reeled. He didn't like how it had made him feel to hear Nessa speak those words to that woman. *He's not an animal.* She'd looked ferocious, disgusted on his behalf. She'd had a similar expression on her face when she'd defended her brother so vociferously when they first met.

It impacted Luc in a very visceral way to think of Nessa standing up for him. He didn't need any of that.

He looked at her now and she was pale. His voice was harsh. 'You didn't need to say that. I can fight my own battles.'

She looked at him. 'She was talking about you as if you're not even human. How could you have ever been with her? She's awful.'

Luc felt disgust move through him. 'We were never lovers, even though she did everything in her power to seduce me. She's Leo Fouret's wife. I found her naked in my bed one night and she threatened to accuse me of rape if I refused to sleep with her. That's why I had to leave the stables. Leo Fouret knew what she was like and he offered to pay me off to leave and say nothing. I refused his money but I did take a horse.'

And why the hell had he just let all of that slip out? He didn't owe Nessa any explanations.

Nessa said slowly, 'That's why you reacted the way you did when you found me in your room.'

She continued, 'I'm sorry I opened my mouth but I couldn't help myself. You're *not* just some object.'

No one had ever jumped to Luc's defence before. A disturbing warmth curled through his gut. His anger was draining away. He said, 'In the end she actually did me a favour. If I hadn't had to leave Fouret's stables I might still be working there. That horse became my fortune.'

Nessa shook her head. 'I don't think so. I think you would have always made your fortune.'

Luc looked at her intently. 'You're like a fierce tigress.'

Nessa's cheeks got hot. She didn't know how to respond to that. She regretted letting that woman get to her, but the relief she felt to know that he hadn't been intimate with Celeste was almost overwhelming.

A thousand more questions were on Nessa's lips but then Luc said, 'You did well this evening.'

Nessa shrugged slightly, embarrassed. 'I felt like a bit of a fraud, to be honest. A couple of well-run races does not merit all that attention.'

Luc shook his head. 'You have a natural ability that anyone can see from a million miles away, and you're a beautiful young woman. It's quite a combination.'

She smiled wryly. 'I've been riding in races for a few years now and no one has ever commented before. I think the fact that I'm riding for you is the key. People are fascinated by whatever you do.'

Luc's jaw tightened. 'Fascinated in that way that

drivers are when they pass a crash and have to look at the carnage.'

Nessa instinctively wanted to deny that but she knew he wasn't saying it for effect or sympathy. She'd seen how the guests had looked at him all evening. And no wonder, with that woman in their midst. It had to be exhausting, constantly having to prove himself.

Afraid he might see too much on her face, Nessa looked out of the window. They were driving along the Seine and Nessa noticed all the amorous couples. It tugged on a yearning inside her.

She couldn't imagine Luc stopping the car and taking her by the hand to walk along the Seine, and it shook her to realise she'd even thought of that. Whatever was between them wasn't about romance or emotions or love. But even as Nessa thought of that word, *love*, her heart pounded unevenly and she felt cold and clammy. Sick.

Oh, God. She was falling for him.

'Have you ever been to Paris before?'

Nessa jumped at his question and looked at him. *She wasn't in love with him. She couldn't be.* She forced down the panic she was feeling, assuring herself that the romance of Paris had infected her brain momentarily.

She said, 'Only once, a long time ago, on a school trip. I always wanted to come back some day—I've never seen anywhere more beautiful.'

Luc's gaze narrowed on Nessa's face. She'd been

a million miles away just now, gazing wistfully out of the window.

His body was in an agony of sexual frustration after an evening standing by her side as countless people, mainly men, he'd noticed, had come and stared as if they'd never seen a woman before. He'd had to control the urge to snarl at everyone so he could pull Nessa into a quiet corner and muss up that far too tidy chignon and peel that dress from her luscious body.

And even though all he wanted right now was to drive straight to his apartment so he could do just that, he found himself leaning forward and instructing his driver to take a small detour.

Nessa looked at him when they came to a stop a few minutes later, after climbing the winding narrow streets as far as they could go in the car. 'Where are we?' she asked.

Luc was already regretting the impetuous decision even as he said, 'Montmartre. Come on, I want to show you something.'

He got out of the car and came around to help her out. Her hand slipped into his, and he had to grit his jaw at the surge of desire even that small, chaste touch provoked.

They walked the small distance up towards Sacre Coeur cathedral. It was late but there were still small knots of people milling around. Luc opened his bow tie and the top button of his shirt. He noticed Nessa shiver slightly in the cool evening air. He took off his jacket and draped it over her shoulders and she looked at him. 'Oh, thank you.'

They came around a corner and the full majesty of the iconic cathedral was revealed. Nessa stopped in her tracks. 'Wow. I'd forgotten this existed. It's so beautiful.'

'You came here on your trip?'

Nessa nodded, her eyes gleaming. 'Yes, but not like this. It's magical.'

He led her around to the front and then down the steps to the lookout points. Nessa sucked in an audible breath. Paris was laid out before them like a glittering carpet of jewels.

Luc realised how long it had been since he'd been here.

'This is stunning. Thank you.'

Luc was ridiculously pleased, which was ironic because over the years he'd presented women with far more tangible and expensive trinkets and had felt nothing when they'd expressed gratitude.

He gestured towards the view. 'I used to come here when I was younger, around age ten, eleven. We'd come in from the flats during the summer, peak tourist season. We used to take advantage of people's absorption with the view to pick their pockets, steal watches, that kind of thing.'

She turned to face him. His coat making her look even more petite, her hair a dramatic splash of red against the night sky.

'Were you ever caught?'

He shook his head. 'That's why they sent us in at that age. We were small and fast, able to disappear in seconds.'

'Who would send you in?'

'The gangs, older kids. We'd bring the haul back to them and if we'd creamed anything off for ourselves they'd know immediately.'

'So you grew up in the suburbs?'

Luc looked out over the city that had been witness to his single-minded ascent out of his grim circumstances. He nodded. 'Where I grew up is about as far removed as you can get from this view. It was a basic existence in not very pretty surroundings. School was a joke and gang life on the streets was our education.'

He looked at her, expecting to see that gleam women got in their eyes when they spied an opening to invite further intimacies but she just looked at him steadily. 'Is that when you got your scar?'

Luc's insides clenched when he remembered the stinging pain. He nodded. 'A rival gang surrounded me, and knives came out. I was lucky to escape with just a scar.' That had been the moment he'd realised that if he didn't get out, he might die.

'You said before that you had no family—did you really have no one?'

Luc's chest tightened. 'My mother died of an overdose when I was sixteen, and my father appeared for the first and last time to get a handout once he saw that I had money. I had no brothers, no sisters. No aunts, uncles, or cousins. So, no, there was no one.'

'Except for Pierre Fortin,' Nessa said quietly.

The tightness in Luc's chest increased. 'Yes. Pierre saved me. He died shortly after I'd received the beating that led to the scar and I took his advice to get out and contact Leo Fouret. If I hadn't done that, I think I might be dead by now.'

Nessa shivered at that. She could tell he wasn't being melodramatic. 'I'm sorry he's gone.' Her voice was husky.

He turned then to face her and for a second there was an expression of such rawness on his face that she was surprised he was letting her see it. And then he reached out and rubbed his knuckles along her jaw. Her breathing quickened in an instant.

'You're very sweet, Nessa O'Sullivan, or else you're a better actress than I've ever seen in my life.'

A sharp pain lanced her to think that even now he still distrusted her. She took her chin away, afraid of the emotion clogging her throat. 'I *am* sorry for your loss. You deserved to have someone in your corner and I'm glad he was there for you.'

Nessa felt exposed but refused to break eye contact. She was determined to show Luc her sincerity even if she had to brand it onto his brain through sheer will.

And then he reached for her, hands sliding under her arms and tugging her towards him until their bodies were flush and she could feel his arousal pressing against her.

Instantly words were forgotten. She got a sense of

how much he'd been leashing his desire all evening and bizarrely felt comforted. Because he'd seemed completely in control and unaffected. But he hadn't been. He was just better at disguising it.

He said, 'I think we've talked enough. I've wanted to do this all evening.'

Before she could ask *what*, he'd started taking the pins out of her hair, until the heavy mass fell down around her shoulders and he dropped the pins to the ground.

He ran his hands through her hair and then cupped her face, tilting it up to his. In the split second before their mouths met, Nessa felt something incredibly poignant move through her as she realised she was one of those kissing couples she'd been so envious of earlier. And then Luc's mouth was on hers, his tongue was mating with hers and she could only clutch at his shirt to try and stay standing. She wasn't even aware of his jacket falling to the ground from her shoulders. She was burning up.

After long, drugging moments Luc pulled back and emitted a curse. 'I could take you right here, right now, but next time we make love it will be on a bed.'

He took her hand to lead her back the way they'd come, to the car. She grabbed his jacket up off the ground as they went, and her cheeks burned. If Luc had decided to make love to her there and then against that wall, she wouldn't have had the ability to stop him.

When they returned to the apartment Luc gave her no time to think. He led her straight to his bedroom. There was one small light burning in the corner, throwing everything into long shadows. His face was stark with need. Exactly how she felt.

He pushed his jacket off her shoulders to the ground and instructed, 'Turn around.'

She turned around, presenting him with her back. He pushed her hair to one side so that it fell over one shoulder, and then he pulled the zip down all the way to where it ended just above her buttocks. He undid her bra. She shivered with anticipation as he ran the knuckles of his fingers up and down her spine.

Then he pushed the two sides of the dress off her shoulders and down and it fell away from her chest. He turned her around again and peeled off her arms so that she was naked from the waist up.

Her nipples stiffened under his gaze, and when he brushed his fingers across the sensitised tips she had to bite her lip to stop from crying out.

He took his hand away. 'Undress me.'

Luc saw the almost drugged expression on Nessa's face. Sweat broke out on his brow at the effort it was taking not to rip the rest of Nessa's dress off her body, throw her onto the bed and sink himself so deep inside her he'd see stars. He had to exert some control before he lost it completely.

She lifted her hands to his shirt and undid each button with an air of concentration that he found curiously touching, tongue trapped between her teeth.

She pushed his shirt off and put her hands to his belt, then the button, and the zip. He was so hard he hurt. When she pushed his trousers down he stepped out of them.

'Your dress and panties. Take them off.' He sounded as rough as he felt, uncouth and desperate.

She pushed the dress down and it landed at her feet in a shimmering green pool. Then she pushed down her panties, revealing the enticing red-gold curls between her legs. She was blushing and not meeting his eye. He tipped up her chin until her eyes met his. 'You're beautiful, Nessa.'

'If you say so.'

'I do. Lie down on the bed.'

She crawled onto the bed and Luc bit back a groan at the sight. Then she lay down on her back. 'Open your legs.'

Shyly she did so and he could see where she glistened with arousal. It undid him. Luc tore off his own underwear and put his hands to her thighs, pushing them apart even more. He knelt between her legs and the scent of her almost drove him wild.

He kissed her inner thighs, and they quivered under his hands. Then he spread apart the lips of her sex and put his mouth to her, getting drunk on her essence. He'd never tasted anything sweeter.

She was moaning and trying to speak. 'Luc, what are you…? *Oh, God.*'

He smiled against her when he could feel the way her body was responding: melting, shivering, tensing. He was remorseless, ignoring her pleas to stop, but not stop. He thrust a finger inside her and she orgasmed around it, muscles clamping down so hard that he had to exert every ounce of self-control not to explode himself.

He sheathed himself and came over her. She looked up at him, dreamy and unfocused. 'That was…incredible.'

For a second, in spite of the raging hunger inside him, Luc stopped. There was something so open and unguarded in her eyes that he couldn't bear it. He felt as if she was looking all the way into the depths of his soul with that steady gaze—in a way no one had ever looked at him before. She was seeing too much.

'Turn over,' he commanded. When she blinked and a look of hesitancy came over her face he felt a sharp tug in his chest. He ignored it. Pushed it down.

He ran his hand down her body, cupping between her legs where she was so damp and hot and fragrant. 'Turn over, *minou*.'

She did and Luc pulled her back until she was on her knees. The delicate curve of her spine and buttocks was breaking him in two. She looked at him over her shoulder in an unconsciously erotic pose. 'Luc?'

He put his hands on her hips and pulled her right into his body. He saw her eyes widen and flare when he pressed against her. And then he was breaching her body as slowly as he could afford to go without going mad, feeling her snug muscles clamp around him and then relax to let him push deeper and deeper.

She let out a low groan, coming down on her elbows, bowing her head. Her hair was a bright fall of red against the white sheets. He saw her curl her hands to fists in the sheets, knuckles white as he drove into her again and again.

But as Luc could feel Nessa's body quickening towards her climax, he felt hollow inside. His own release was elusive. He realised he couldn't do it like this, no matter how exposed the other way made him feel. He pulled out, his whole body screaming in protest.

He turned Nessa around again so she was on her back. She was panting, skin gleaming with perspiration. 'Luc...'

'Look at me.'

She did, her eyes wide and trusting. Desperate for the release that he was withholding. He thrust into her again, just once, and that was all it took to send them both hurtling over the edge.

When Luc was capable of movement again he pulled free of Nessa's embrace, and went into his bathroom to dispense with the protection. He placed his hands on the sink and bowed his head. He felt momentarily weak, as if some of his strength had been drained away during sex.

He grimaced at the fanciful notion of Samson and

Delilah. It was just the after-effects of extreme pleasure. *But,* a small voice reminded him, *you weren't able to climax until you were looking in her eyes. You needed that connection.* Luc had never sought that kind of connection before.

He went cold. The events of the evening flooded his mind and an icy finger danced down his spine.

He'd told Nessa more than he'd told anyone. He'd blithely let most of his sad history trip off his tongue without a moment's hesitation. He went even icier when the full significance of that hit him.

He'd lost sight of who she was. And what she could *still* be: an accessory to theft.

A hard knot formed in his gut. He'd become so blinded by lust for her that he'd lost sight of a lifetime of lessons, teaching him to trust no one. Luc's heart beat fast to think of how close he'd come to— He shut that thought down. He didn't trust her. They'd had sex. That was all.

He had to admit that since she'd been riding for him, the turnaround in public perception was phenomenal. That was the important thing here. Not his lust for her. That was a base instinct he couldn't afford to indulge again.

He also had to acknowledge the fact that, in spite of the reasons why she was there, she was a boon to his business. But she owed him this. Her brother had stolen from him and she had taken on the debt for herself.

A familiar feeling of ruthlessness settled over Luc

like a well-worn coat. In spite of Nessa's innocence or apparent sweetness, he still couldn't trust that she wasn't taking advantage of his desire for her.

He would not be weak again.

CHAPTER NINE

NESSA COULD HEAR Luc in the bathroom. The shower was turned on. She opened her eyes in the dim light of the bedroom, unable to stop imagining water sluicing down over that powerful body. Between her legs ached pleasurably as she recalled the breathtaking feeling of Luc's body driving into hers over and over again.

She got hot when she thought of how he'd made her turn over, taking her from behind. There'd been something so raw and animalistic about it. It had also felt erotic, but she'd felt slightly unsure, out of her depth. She hadn't liked not being able to see his face, or his eyes. Until he'd turned her back and said *look at me*, and that was all it had taken to send her shattering into a million pieces.

The bathroom door opened and Nessa instinctively pulled the sheet up over her body, suddenly shy, which was ridiculous after what had just happened.

Luc stood in the doorway with nothing but a small

towel hooked around his waist. Droplets of moisture clung to his sculpted muscles and Nessa's mouth watered.

'You should go back to your own bed now.'

Nessa sat up, holding the sheet to her chest. Humiliation rushed through her. Of course. What had she expected would happen? That Luc would come back to bed and take her in his arms again, whisper sweet nothings in her ears and want to cuddle?

'I don't sleep with lovers,' he said, as if he might not have been clear enough.

Nessa looked at him, unable to stem the blooming of hurt inside her. 'It's fine. You don't need to explain.'

She scooted to the side of the bed feeling awkward as well as humiliated as she searched for her dress, which lay on the ground a few feet away in a pool of shimmering green. She was just wondering how to get there without exposing herself even further when Luc appeared in her eyeline holding out a robe.

'Here.' He sounded gruff.

Nessa took it and pulled it on while trying to stay as covered up as possible. She hated herself for feeling so hurt by Luc's dismissal, by the confirmation that she was no different from his other lovers. *But you want to be different.* She stood up, belting the robe around her, squashing that thought. She didn't want to be different. *Yes, you do.*

Before Luc might see any evidence of the tumult of her emotions, Nessa plucked the dress up off the floor and walked to the door, avoiding his eye. She forced herself to stop, though, and turned around. 'Thank you for this evening. I had a nice time.'

Nessa had walked out of the door before Luc had a chance to respond. He waited for a sense of satisfaction that he'd made it clear that he had boundaries, but it wouldn't come. He thought of how awkward she'd looked just now at the door, avoiding his eye, clutching her dress. She wasn't like the women he knew. He felt like a heel now. Not satisfied at all.

If he was brutally honest with himself, he already regretted saying anything. He wanted to go after her, bring her back to bed and continue where they'd finished.

Luc bit off a savage curse and went back into the bathroom to take a cold shower. Damn Nessa O'Sullivan for sliding under his skin like this. The sooner his people tracked down her brother, the better.

Nessa couldn't sleep when she went back to her bedroom. She went out to the balcony and sat on the chair by the small table, looking at the view. She was such a naive fool. To have imagined for a second that Luc's opening up to her earlier that evening had meant anything.

It had meant nothing. He'd been on a trip down memory lane and she'd happened to be there.

It hit her then, with a cold, clammy sense of panic. She really was falling for him, and it was already too late. She had stood up for him in front of Celeste Fouret the way she would stand up for any of her loved ones. The thought that Luc might have interpreted her defence as devotion, and that had been why he'd sent her back to her own room, made her feel nauseous.

She knew now, with an awful sense of impending doom, that whatever emotional pain she thought she'd ever felt before would pale into insignificance once this man cast her aside. As surely he would.

Because Celeste Fouret had been right, after all. Luc Barbier would never belong to anyone. And certainly not Nessa. She was a brief interlude. A novelty for a cynical and jaded man, and she knew now that she had to protect herself before she got in any deeper.

The following morning Nessa got washed, dressed and packed before going in search of Luc. She heard movement coming from the main living area and walked into the room to see the dining table set and the housekeeper serving breakfast.

Sunlight streamed through the huge windows but it all paled into insignificance next to the image of Luc wearing a dark suit, sipping coffee and reading a newspaper, clean shaven. He looked every inch a titan of industry, and as remote as a rock in the middle of the ocean.

His dark glance barely skimmed over her, and Nessa was glad as it would give her the strength to do what she knew she had to for her own self-preservation.

Lucille told her to take a seat and that she'd bring her some breakfast. Nessa smiled her thanks, relieved that she wasn't entirely alone with Luc.

He put down the paper as she sat down. She felt self-conscious in her daily uniform of jeans and a T-shirt. She'd hung the glittering dress back up in the closet and had pushed down the dangerous spurt of emotion when she remembered Luc telling her she was beautiful.

'Did you sleep well?'

She looked at him and it almost hurt, he was so gorgeous. She nodded and told a white lie. 'Very well, thank you. Your apartment is beautiful. You're very lucky.'

Lucille came back and placed a plate down in front of Nessa with perfectly fluffy scrambled eggs with spring onions, salmon and buttered toast. Ordinarily her mouth would have watered but for some reason she felt nauseous. Not wanting to insult the Frenchwoman, she spooned a mouthful and ate, murmuring her appreciation to the beaming woman. When they were alone again Nessa put down her fork and took a sip of coffee, willing the faint nausea away.

Luc said, 'Luck had nothing to do with me having this apartment. It was success born out of hard work.'

Nessa shouldn't have been surprised that Luc didn't believe in things like luck, or chance. She hadn't either for a long time after their mother's death had rent their world apart. Until fate had stepped in, bringing Nadim into her sister's life, transforming their fortunes.

The hurt she still felt made her want to pierce a little of Luc's stark black and white attitude. 'Well, I do believe in luck. I believe there's always a moment when fate intervenes and you can choose to take advantage of it or not. Not everything is within our control.'

Luc's mouth tightened. 'Apparently not.'

Nessa wasn't sure what that meant. Incensed now, she said, 'Don't you consider Pierre Fortin to have been fateful for you?'

Luc looked at her. 'He gave me an opportunity and I made the most of it.'

Nessa resisted making a face at Luc's obduracy and made a stab at eating some more of the delicious breakfast, and tried to ignore the churning of her stomach.

Luc said, 'I have some meetings to attend in Paris today. My driver will take you to my stables just outside the city this morning, where you'll meet with François, my head trainer. He's expecting you. He'll see how you go on Sur La Mer and, depending on what he thinks, you'll ride him in the race next week. Or not.'

Nessa put down her fork. 'What if I don't perform well on Sur La Mer?'

Luc shrugged minutely. 'Then you'll go back to the stables in Ireland.'

She felt like a pawn being moved about at Luc's will. Into his bed, out of it…it was time to claim back her independence. She took a deep breath.

'Luc, I—'

'Look, Nessa—'

They both spoke at the same moment and stopped. Luc said, 'You go.'

Nessa's heart hammered. She swallowed. 'I just wanted to say that I don't think we should sleep together again. I'm here to do a job. I'd like to focus on that.'

Luc looked at her, eyes glittering like two black unreadable jewels. She'd never know what this man was thinking in a million years. He was too well protected. As she should be.

'I agree. I was going to say the same thing.'

'That's good,' Nessa said quickly, even as something curled up inside her. Some very pathetic part of her that had hoped that he might refuse to agree.

Then Luc stood up and walked over to the window. Nessa stood too, still feeling that nausea in her stomach. It got worse.

He turned around, hands in his pockets. 'As you said, you're here to focus on a job, a job that you've proven to have a great talent for. That's the most important thing now.'

Of course it was, because it was bringing the Barbier name respect and success. And as Nessa had learnt, Luc's business and reputation were everything to him. She couldn't begrudge him that. Not after everything he'd been through. But it was clear that he had no interest in anything outside that. Certainly not a personal life, with love, fulfilment, or family.

As if reading her mind, he said, 'My life isn't about relationships, Nessa. I don't have anything to offer you except what we've shared. There are other women who understand that and can accept it. You're different and, believe me, that's a good thing. But I don't do fairy-tale endings. For me…the novelty has worn off.'

The novelty has worn off. The sheen had gone from his naive virginal lover. Nessa should be thanking him for being so brutally honest, but she just felt incredibly sad, and sick.

She lifted her chin. 'I'm not as naive as you might think, Luc. And I don't believe in fairy tales either.' *Liar…* whispered that voice. Nessa ignored it.

'I'm ready to leave now, if you want to let your driver know.'

For a long moment there was silence and Nessa felt tension rise in the room. Eventually Luc said, 'Of course, I'll call him now and let him know you're coming down.'

So polite. So civil. So devastating. *So over.*

Nessa turned and left the room and when she reached her own bathroom she couldn't keep the nausea down any longer. She looked at herself in the mirror afterwards and saw how pale she was.

It was time to get a grip on herself again and for-get anything had happened between her and Luc. Do the race, win the money, pay off Paddy's debt. That was her focus now. Nothing else.

Four days later Nessa was tired and aching all over from training so hard. François appeared at the door to Sur La Mer's stall where Nessa was rubbing him down and trying hard *not* to let her mind deviate with humiliating predictability to Luc Barbier.

She'd almost hoped that when she first sat on Sur La Mer, he'd throw her off. But he'd been a dream to ride and she'd connected with him immediately. François had been ecstatic.

Luc hadn't appeared once at the gallops to watch them train, but then one of the other jockeys had pointed to the CCTV cameras and told her that Luc often watched remotely from screens in his office.

Nessa knew he was at the stables because he'd returned from Paris the day after she'd arrived. The thought that he was watching her progress but avoiding any more personal dealings with her slid through her ribs like a knife, straight to her heart.

François was looking at her as if waiting for a response and Nessa blushed to have been caught out daydreaming. 'I'm sorry, did you want me for something?'

'It's Luc—he wants to see you in his office. It's in the main house on the first floor.'

The roiling in her gut intensified. The ever-present nausea that never seemed to quit. Nessa dusted her hands off and patted Sur La Mer before following François back out, careful to lock the stall door behind her.

He left her at the main door of the house and she went in, making her way up to Luc's office. The door was closed and she took a deep breath, hating that she felt so jittery and on edge at the thought of seeing him again.

She knocked lightly.

'Come in.'

She pushed the door open and Luc was standing behind his desk in jeans and a T-shirt. For a moment Nessa felt so dizzy and light-headed she thought she might faint. She clutched the doorknob like a lifeline.

'You wanted to see me?'

It was only then that she noticed he was on the phone. And he looked grim. He held the receiver towards her. 'It's Paddy.'

For a second she just looked at him. Her brain felt sluggish. 'Paddy...?'

Now he looked impatient. 'Your brother.'

Nessa moved forward feeling as if she were under water. Weighed down. It was shock. She took the phone and Paddy's familiar voice came down the line. 'Ness? Are you there?'

Luc moved away to the window.

Nessa turned away to hide the tears blurring her vision to hear her brother's familiar voice. 'Paddy, where are you? What's going on?'

Her brother sounded happy. 'Ness, it's all been cleared up. Well, not the money, I'll still owe Mr

Barbier but he knows now it wasn't my fault. He's agreed to give me my job back and I'll start paying him back out of my wages every month. I'm going to do a course in cyber security too so we can prevent this happening again. He told me you're riding for him in a big race tomorrow—that's fantastic news, Ness! Look, I've got to run. I'm catching a flight home tonight. I'll call you when I get back and tell you everything. Love you, Ness.'

And the phone connection went dead. It was all over, just like that.

She looked at the phone for a long moment trying to gather herself and when she felt a bit more composed she turned around. Luc was standing in front of his window, arms folded. Nessa put the phone receiver back in the cradle.

She forced herself to meet his gaze. 'Can you tell me what's going on?'

He was still grim. 'It was Gio Corretti who realised what was happening, because it happened to him with another horse. Someone had hacked into his computer system so they could impersonate Gio's stud manager. They would then say something about a slight change in bank account details and the buyer would send the money to the hacker's account. That's what happened to Paddy. He'd suspected something, but by the time he'd figured out what had happened the money was gone and couldn't be traced. Then he panicked.'

Luc continued, 'Shortly after speaking to Gio

Corretti, my security firm tracked Paddy down to the United States. He was staying with your twin brother.'

Nessa flushed with guilt.

Luc continued, 'I got in touch with Paddy to let him know he could come back. I told him never to do such a foolhardy thing like running away from a problem again.'

Nessa could feel Luc's barely leashed anger and almost felt sorry for her brother.

Luc unfolded his arms then and ran a hand through his hair. Nessa realised it was messier than usual and he looked tired. Stubble lined his jaw. She felt a spurt of pain when she wondered if he'd already taken a replacement into his bed. Someone whose novelty wouldn't wear off so quickly. Someone who knew the rules. Someone who didn't want the fairy tale.

He put his hands on his hips and looked at her. 'Obviously you're now free to go. I'd like you to run the race tomorrow on Sur La Mer but if you'd prefer not to, I will accept that. It's only fair. You have no obligation to me any more.'

Nessa blinked. She hadn't considered that. She felt a little panicky. 'But what about Paddy's debt? He said he still has to pay that back.'

'I told him the debt would be forgiven but he's insisting on paying it back for having been lax enough to be taken in by the hackers. Nothing I said would make him change his mind.'

Nessa's heart squeezed. Luc had been prepared to let the debt go. One million euros.

She made a decision, even though a part of her wanted nothing more than to turn around and walk away right now and go somewhere private where she could lick her wounds and try to get on with her life. She had to be professional about this and the race tomorrow was a huge opportunity for her.

'I'll run the race tomorrow. But if I win, or place, and there's any prize money I'd still like it to go towards the debt.'

'You wouldn't take it for yourself?'

Nessa shook her head. 'No. I don't want anything. I don't need anything from you. Are we done here?'

Every bone in Nessa's body ached with the need to be closer to this man. Have him touch her. It was agony.

Eventually Luc said, 'Yes, we're done.'

Nessa turned and walked to the door, but at the last second he called her name. For a heart-stopping moment she thought she'd heard some inflection in his voice and she couldn't control the surge of hope.

But when she turned around he was expressionless. He said, 'Wherever you go, or whatever you want to do in the future, you'll have my endorsement. I would retain you as a jockey at my stables here or in Ireland but I don't think you would welcome working for me.'

The thought of working alongside Luc Barbier

every day for years to come, and seeing him lead his life as the lone wolf that he was, taking and discarding women as he went, was unthinkable. And it just drove home how unaffected by her he was.

She lifted her chin. 'Frankly, after tomorrow, Luc, I hope I never see you again.'

The following day before the race, Nessa was sick with nerves. Literally. Her breakfast had just ended up in the toilet bowl of the ladies' changing room at the racetrack. She cursed Luc Barbier as the source of all her ills and forced herself to just concentrate on getting through the race in one piece.

She'd booked herself on a flight back to Dublin later that night. Soon this would all be behind her.

She weighed out and made her way to the starting gate to line up with the rest of the horses and jockeys. She was oblivious to their curious looks. They were led into the stalls one by one. One horse started kicking and it took about three men to get him into position.

As Nessa waited on Sur La Mer, feeling his restlessness underneath her, she pushed all thoughts of anything else but the task at hand out of her head.

She took a deep breath. And then the gate snapped open and she unleashed the power of the horse beneath her.

As was becoming a familiar refrain, François said beside Luc, 'I don't believe it. She's going to win, Luc.'

An immense surge of pride and something much more tangled made Luc's chest swell and grow tight.

He watched as Nessa approached the last furlong, moving through the air like a comet. She looked tiny on the horse and something else moved through him, stark and unpleasant. Fear, for her safety.

When she'd stood before him in his office the day before, it had taken all of his control not to drag her into his bedroom like a Neanderthal and strap her to his bed so she could never leave.

He was going mad. She wasn't out of his system. His system burned for her. But it was too late. This was it. She'd be gone within hours. *I hope I never see you again.*

He'd ruthlessly contemplated seducing her again, but he knew he couldn't do it. Much to his own surprise, it would appear he did have something of a conscience. Nessa wasn't like the other women. She was strong, yes, but soft. Her eyes held nothing back. She might say she didn't believe in fairy tales but he knew that, in spite of the obvious trauma of her mother's death and its effect on their family, there was still something hopeful about her.

She deserved someone who could nurture that hope. Never before had Luc been made so aware of his malfunctioning emotions.

But, as much as he could tell himself that he was doing this to protect her, he had the insidious suspicion that it was also himself he was protecting. He wasn't even sure from what, though.

'Luc, *look*! She's won!'

Luc saw Nessa shoot past the post and the usual sense of achievement and triumph when one of his horses won was tinged with something darker. '*Merde*, Luc, that horse is out of control...'

Luc went cold. He saw the other horses thundering over the line and spotted one that was riderless. It was going berserk. And it was heading straight for Nessa, who had slowed down and was turning around. Even from here Luc could see the huge smile on her face. A tendril of red hair falling from under her cap. Everyone was cheering.

But it was as if he were stuck under water and everything happened in slow motion. He saw the riderless horse rear up in front of Sur La Mer. Another jockey, still on his horse, tried to calm that horse down, but Nessa somehow got stuck in the middle. Sur La Mer bucked. There was a blur of movement, a huge collective gasp from the crowd and Nessa was off the horse and lying on the ground. Underneath the three horses.

Luc wasn't even aware he'd vaulted over the fence. All he could see was a horrifying tangle of horseflesh, hooves, and Nessa inert underneath it all.

The ambulance and paramedics were attending her by the time he got there and he only realised someone was holding him back when François' voice broke through the pounding of blood in his head.

'Luc! Leave them alone. They're doing all they can. Sur La Mer is fine. Someone has him.'

* * *

'I'm afraid I can only give out information to family or loved ones, Mr Barbier.'

Loved ones. That struck Luc forcibly, but he pushed down its significance. He was desperate to know if Nessa was all right and her family weren't here. *No,* said a voice, *because you took her away from them.*

Luc ignored the admonishing voice, and his growing sense of guilt. 'I'm not just her employer. We've been lovers.'

The doctor looked at him suspiciously for a moment but there must have been some expression on Luc's face because then he said, 'Very well. If you're intimately acquainted, then there's something you should know. Injury-wise, she was a very lucky young woman. She escaped from under those horses with just a badly bruised back. It could have been a lot worse.'

Luc felt sick when he thought of how much worse it could have been, how vulnerable she'd looked.

The doctor sighed heavily. 'However, there was something else. I'm afraid we weren't able to save the baby. She wasn't even aware she was pregnant so I'm guessing it's news to you too. It was very early—just a few weeks. There's no way of saying for sure why the miscarriage happened; it could have been the shock and trauma, but equally it could have just been one of those things. Having said that, there's no reason why she can't get pregnant again and have a perfectly healthy baby.'

* * *

Luc stood outside the hospital a few minutes later, barely aware of the glances he was drawing. He was reeling. In shock. *Pregnant. A baby.*

He couldn't breathe with the knowledge that he'd almost had a family and in the same moment it was gone.

He'd spent so long telling himself a family wasn't for him that it was utterly shocking now to find himself feeling such an acute sense of…loss and grief.

He'd only ever felt like this a couple of times in his life. When he'd found his mother's dead body, and when Pierre Fortin had died. He'd vowed to himself he'd never let anyone close enough to hurt him again.

But this caught him unawares, blindsiding him.

The grief he felt for this tiny unborn child told him he'd been lying to himself for a long time. He'd blocked out the thought of children, not because of his own miserable upbringing, but because of the potential pain of losing someone again.

He might have believed he'd crushed the dream of a family. But it had remained, like a little kernel inside him. Immune to his cynicism. Immune to his attempts to control his life by creating so much wealth and success that he would never feel at the mercy of his environment again.

Family. Nessa had been pregnant with his child, and she'd almost died under those horses' hooves. He felt clammy at the thought of how close she'd come to serious injury. She'd been pregnant with his child because of *his* lack of care in protecting them both. She was his family now, in spite of the loss of the baby.

The doctor's words came back: *there's no reason why she can't get pregnant again.*

There, on the steps of the hospital, Luc was aware of his whole world view changing. The vision he'd always had for his life and legacy had been far too narrow. He could see that now.

Everything had just changed in an instant and he knew there was only one way forward.

Nessa was one big throbbing ache that radiated out from her back and all over her body, but most acutely in her womb. The place where her baby had been. A baby she hadn't even been aware of.

It was a particularly cruel and unusual thing to be told you're pregnant, and, in the same breath, that you're not.

How could she be feeling so much for something that had been so ephemeral? *Because it was Luc's. And because you do want the fairy tale. And because as soon as the doctor told you you'd been pregnant, you pictured a small child with dark hair. A child who would grow up secure and loved and who would take all of that dark cynicism out of his eyes. A child who would take away the terror you've always felt at the thought of your world collapsing around you again...*

Nessa squeezed her eyes shut at the surge of emotion that gripped her. She felt a tear leak out. But before she could wipe it away there was the sound of the door, and her heart clenched because she knew instantly who it was.

'Nessa.'

She quickly dashed the tear away, keeping her face turned towards the window. When she felt slightly more composed she opened her eyes and turned her head. And she knew straight away that he knew. The doctor had told him.

His suit was crumpled, tie undone, shirt open at the top. He came in and stood near the bed, eyes so dark that Nessa felt as if she might drown in them.

'I didn't know about the baby,' she said, hating the defensive tone in her voice.

'I know.'

The emotional turmoil of the past few hours and weeks and Luc's inscrutability made Nessa lash out. 'Do you? Are you sure I didn't do it on purpose to try and trap you?'

Something fleeting and pained crossed Luc's face but Nessa felt no triumph to have pierced that impenetrable wall. 'Once,' he admitted, 'I might have suspected such a thing but I know you now.'

He did. She'd let him right into the heart of her. And she resisted that now even though it was far too late. 'No, you don't. Not really. You have no idea what I want.'

Luc sat down on a chair near the head of the bed and sat forward. Suddenly he was too close.

'What do you want, Nessa?'

You, came the automatic response. She looked away from that hard-boned face. 'I want you to leave, Luc. My brother is coming from Dublin to help take me home first thing tomorrow.'

She heard a curse and movement and the bed dipped as Luc sat down. Nessa couldn't move without extreme pain so she was trapped. She glared at him, seizing on as much anger and pain as she could to protect herself.

He looked fierce. 'We just lost a baby, Nessa. We need to talk about this.'

More pain gripped her. '*I* lost a baby, Luc. Don't try to pretend you would have ever welcomed the news.'

He stood up, eyes burning. 'What are you saying? That you would have never told me?'

Nessa was taken aback. 'I don't know. I didn't have to make that decision.'

'Would you have got rid of it?'

Nessa's hands automatically went to her belly and the answer was immediate and instinctive. '*No.*'

Luc seemed to relax slightly. He paced away from the bed for a moment, running his hand through his hair. Nessa's gaze couldn't help taking in his unconsciously athletic grace, even now.

He turned to face her again. 'I won't pretend I wasn't shocked by the news, and I can't blame you for thinking I wouldn't welcome it. I've never made any secret of the fact I don't want to have a family. I never wanted to be a father because my own was absent, so how would I know what to do?

'But now,' he said, 'things are different.'

Nessa's mouth was suddenly dry and her heart thumped. 'What do you mean?'

She had no warning for when Luc said in a very determined tone, 'I think we should get married.'

CHAPTER TEN

NESSA JUST LOOKED at Luc in shock. Finally she asked, 'Are you sure you didn't receive a head injury?'

He shook his head. He stood at the end of the bed, hands on the rail. 'I'm serious, Nessa. We would be having a very different conversation right now if you hadn't lost the baby.'

Sharp pain lanced her. 'Do you think it was my fault? I didn't know... I felt nauseous all last week but I thought it was just—' She stopped. She'd thought it was due to emotional turmoil. Not pregnancy.

Luc came and sat down near the bed again. 'No, Nessa. Of course it wasn't your fault. The doctor said these things happen. But the fact is that we almost had a baby and if you *were* pregnant there is no way we wouldn't be getting married. No child of mine will be born out of wedlock. I was born that way and I won't inflict the same unsure existence on my child.'

Nessa was desperately trying to read Luc, to absorb what he was saying. 'But I'm not pregnant, so why on earth would you want to marry me?'

As if he couldn't be contained, Luc got up and paced again. He stopped. 'Because this experience has made me face up to the fact that I'm not as averse to the thought of family as I thought I was. Having a child, an heir, it's something I'd always rejected. But I can see the benefits now.'

Nessa shrank back into the pillows. 'That all sounds very clinical.'

Luc came to the end of the bed again. 'I would love it to the best of my ability. I would give it a good life, every opportunity. Brothers, sisters. Like your family.'

It. Something in Nessa shrivelled up.

'What about me?' she forced herself to ask. 'Would you love me to the best of your ability?'

He waved a dismissive hand. 'This isn't about love—that's why it would be a success. We'd be going into this with eyes open and no illusions. I still want you, Nessa. And I can offer you a commitment now.'

He went on. 'We're a good team. These last few weeks have been a success for both of us professionally. We can expand on that, create an empire.'

'Just a few days ago you told me *the novelty had worn off.*'

'I didn't want to hurt you.'

'Well, you did,' Nessa said bluntly. She felt sick all over again at this evidence of just how far he was willing to go in a bid to achieve his ultimate ambition.

'As flattered as I am that you would consider me

a good choice to be your wife and mother of your children, I'm afraid I can't accept.'

Luc's brows snapped together. 'Why not?'

'Because I don't love you.' *Liar.*

He didn't miss a beat. 'We don't need love. We have amazing chemistry.'

'Which you said would *fizzle out*,' Nessa pointed out.

A muscle pulsed in Luc's jaw. 'I underestimated our attraction. I don't see it fizzling out any time soon.'

'But it *will*,' Nessa all but wailed. 'And then what? You take mistresses while our children see their parents grow more distant?'

She shook her head. 'I won't do it, Luc. Before my mother died my parents had a blissfully happy marriage. I won't settle for anything less. I'm very pleased for you that you've figured out what you want, but I'm not it. Go and choose one of the women who understand your rules. I'm sure one of them can give you everything you need.'

His words mocked her. *This isn't about love.* But it was. For her. And now that she'd broken her own rules and fallen in love, she knew she couldn't settle for anything less than what her parents had had and what she saw in her sister and brother-in-law's relationship. True selfless devotion. Trust.

Surely that was worth the fear of losing the one you loved? Even knowing that for a short time?

'Nessa—'

'I'm sorry, sir, you'll have to leave. She needs to rest now. Her blood pressure is going up.' A nurse had come in and neither of them had noticed.

Suddenly Nessa felt very weary. 'Luc, just go. And please don't come back. I can't give you what you've decided you need.'

For a long moment she thought he was going to refuse to leave. He looked as if he was about to pluck her from the bed. But then he lifted his hands up in a gesture of surrender. It was a very *un*-Luc gesture. 'I'll go, for now. But this conversation isn't over, Nessa.'

Yes, it is, she vowed silently as she watched him walk out.

The nurse came over and fussed around Nessa, checking her stats. She winked at Nessa and said, 'If you can't give him what he needs, just send him my way.'

Nessa forced a weak smile and laid her head back on the pillow. It was throbbing with everything Luc had just proposed. *Luc had just proposed.* But he hadn't. It wasn't a real proposal. He'd proposed a business merger. No doubt he saw the benefits of being related in marriage to Sheikh Nadim; it would place Luc in an untouchable place. Finally he would have all the respect and social acceptance he craved. And Nessa would be a side benefit of that. His wife, the jockey, who could be trotted out at social events as a star attraction. For as long as she won those races, of course.

And then bear his children, who he'd suddenly decided would be a convenient vehicle to carry on his name.

In a way she envied Luc—that he could be so coolly calculating and detached. She wanted to be detached. Not in love.

The nurse left the room. Just then Nessa's phone rang on the bedside table and she picked it up, expecting it to be Paddy. But it was Iseult, calling from Merkazad. She sounded frantic. 'Ness, what on earth happened? Are you okay?'

Nessa forced it all out of her head and told her sister everything. Everything, except how she'd fallen stupidly in love with Luc Barbier and lost his child.

It had been a week since Luc had seen Nessa in Paris and he'd since returned to the stables in Ireland.

He'd gone back to the hospital the day after their conversation to find her room empty and ready for the next patient. She'd already left for Ireland, with her brother. He'd since found out that her brother-in-law had arranged a private jet for them to go back to Kildare.

The image of Nessa being taken back into the bosom of her protective family was all too vivid for Luc's liking. He hadn't liked the spiking of panic and the feeling of being very, very out of control.

He had to admit now that he'd had it all so very

wrong. Paddy hadn't been a thief, and Nessa hadn't been an accessory. They were just a close-knit family.

Luc hadn't pursued her since then because she needed to recuperate, and he knew she also needed time to go over his proposal.

But there was no way that she was refusing his proposal the next time. Damn the woman anyway. From the very first moment he'd laid eyes on her she'd challenged him, thwarted him and generally behaved in exactly the opposite manner to which he expected. His blood thrummed even now as he looked out over the gallops and expected to see a head of dark red hair glinting in the sunshine.

It was inconceivable that he wouldn't see her here again, that she would turn him down. The chemistry between them was still as strong as ever. He would seduce her, and convince her to agree to his proposal. The alternative was not an option.

'What do you mean she's not at home?'

Luc glared at Paddy, who gulped. Luc had summoned the young man to his office to ask for directions to the O'Sullivan farm. It was time to bring Nessa back.

'She's gone to Merkazad. Iseult needed some help with the new baby. It's due any day now.'

Luc's blood pressure was reaching boiling point. 'But she's injured!'

Paddy looked sheepish. 'She said she felt much better already.'

He could imagine that all too well. Her sister said she needed her, and Nessa jumped, without a thought for herself.

Luc made an inarticulate sound and dismissed Paddy. He paced his office, feeling like a caged animal. He needed Nessa *now*, and she was on the other side of the world.

A cold, clammy sweat broke out on Luc's brow and he stopped dead as the significance of that sank in. *He needed her.* When he'd never needed anyone in his life. Not even Pierre Fortin had impacted Luc as hard, and that man had given him a whole new life.

Luc assured himself now that he just needed her for all the myriad reasons he'd told her that day at the hospital. That was all. But the clammy feeling wouldn't recede.

He went to his drinks cabinet and poured himself a shot of whisky. He felt as if he were unravelling at the seams. He took another shot, but the panic wouldn't go away.

Eventually Luc went outside to the stables and staff scattered as he approached when they saw the look on his face. Pascal bumped into him and stepped back. 'Woah, Luc. What's wrong? Has something happened?'

Luc all but snarled at him and strode off. He went to the stables and saddled up his favourite horse, cantering out of the yard and up into the fields and tracks surrounding his land. He came to a stop only when the horse was lathered in sweat and heaving for breath. Like him.

He slid off the horse and stood by his head, holding the reins. This was the same hill he'd come to when he'd bought this place. He could remember the immense sense of satisfaction to be expanding his empire into one of the world's most respected racing communities. *Finally,* he'd thought then, *I'll be seen as one of them. I'll no longer be tainted by my past.*

But as he stood in exactly the same place now, Luc realised his past was no further away than it ever had been. It was still as vivid as ever. He expected to feel frustration or a sense of futility because he knew now he'd never escape it. He waited, but all he did feel, surprisingly, was a measure of peace.

For the first time, Luc could appreciate that his past had made him who he was and there was a curious sense of pride in that.

Yet, this revelation left a hollow ache inside him because he had no one to share it with. He knew now that there was only one person he would want to share it with, and she was gone. A sense of bleakness gripped him.

Nessa had returned to the protection of *her* home, *her* family, and Luc had no place there. He had no right to claim her. For a brief moment they could have been together, but it had been taken away and he had no right to that dream with her.

She didn't love him, and if he had an ounce of humanity left he would not take advantage of their attraction to persuade her otherwise. She deserved someone far better than he would ever be.

The horse moved restlessly beside him, ready to return home, and Luc felt the bitter sting of irony. He wanted to go home too, but the home he wanted to go to didn't exist, because he'd spent his whole life denying that it could exist, or that he needed it. And now it was too late.

'Nessa, if you had told me about the baby I never would have let you come all the way here.'

Nessa's emotions bubbled up under the sympathetic gaze of her older sister, who was sitting with her in one of Merkazad castle's beautiful courtyards. They'd just been served afternoon tea, which had remained untouched as Nessa had spilled out the last few weeks' events under the expert questioning of her concerned sister, who had noticed something was off.

Much as Nessa might have guessed, Iseult had already vowed to pay off Paddy's debt to Luc Barbier, and Nessa was glad she hadn't told Iseult before now. She would have been far too worried and insisted on getting involved. At least this way it was all over; whether or not Paddy would let Iseult and Nadim take on the debt was for him to deal with now.

'It's fine, Iseult. I'm glad I came. Really.' She adored her nephew, Kamil, a dark-haired imp of five going on twenty-five, who was as excited about the imminent birth as everyone else.

Iseult reached for her hand now, squeezing it gently. 'And what about Luc?'

Nessa sighed. 'What about Luc? He proposed marriage as a business merger, not out of romance or love.'

'But you do love him?'

Nessa desperately wanted to say no. But in the end she nodded, feeling her heart contract with pain.

Her sister sat back again, placing a hand over her rotund bump that looked ready to pop under her kaftan. Just then Kamil burst into the courtyard, holding his palm tablet and saying excitedly, 'Look, Auntie Ness, I found you on the Internet!'

He jumped up onto Nessa's lap and started playing the video of Nessa's last race. Iseult suddenly realised the significance and reached across, saying, 'I don't think Auntie Ness wants to see that one, Kami. Let's find another.'

But Nessa shot a smile at Iseult even as her heart was thumping. 'It's fine. I wouldn't mind seeing it anyway. I haven't looked back at it yet.'

The tablet was propped on the table and Kamil squealed with excitement on Nessa's lap as the race drew to a close and she won.

When Kamil wriggled off her lap to run off again Nessa barely noticed. And she didn't see the concern on her sister's face. Her eyes were glued to the screen and the aftermath of the race. She saw the riderless horse and then a flurry of movement, Sur La Mer bucking and then herself disappearing underneath the horses.

She had no memory of the actual incident, so it was like watching someone else.

A blur of movement entered the frame from the right. A man, pushing his way through, throwing people out of his way and shouting. The camera focused on him, zooming in. Nessa realised with a jolt that it was Luc, and that he was being held back by Francois while the medics cleared a space and worked on her.

Francois was saying something indistinct to him and then Luc turned around with a savage look on his face and shouted very clearly, *'I don't care about the damn horse, I care about her.'*

The video clip stopped then, frozen on Luc's fierce expression.

Nessa looked warily at Iseult, who arched a brow. 'That does not look like a man who is driven by ambition to marry a woman he sees only as a business opportunity, now, does it?'

'He's in the gym on the first floor, love. He's in there for hours in the morning and every evening. It's like he's trying to exorcise the devil himself.'

Nessa smiled her thanks at Mrs Owens. Her heart was palpitating—she'd come here straight from Dublin airport. Iseult had insisted she come home, all but bundling her onto the plane herself saying fiercely, *'You'll always regret it if you don't find out for sure, Ness.'*

Nessa had known herself that even if Luc did feel

something for her, he wouldn't come after her. He'd been too hurt by his past. He'd never had anyone to depend on. Not really. And anyone he'd felt anything for had died.

It had only dawned on Nessa then that they actually had more in common than she'd ever appreciated. Fear of loss. Grief.

The difference was that she'd had a family around her and he'd had no one.

She stopped outside the door to the gym. It was too late to worry about how she looked in worn jeans and a long-sleeved top. No make-up. Hair up in a loose topknot. Impulsively at the last second, she undid it and her hair fell down around her shoulders.

All she could hear from behind the door was a low and muffled-sounding rhythmic *thump thump*.

She took a deep breath and opened the door into the vast room. All Nessa saw at first were a hundred complicated-looking machines. But Luc wasn't on any of those.

He was at the other end of the room punching a heavy bag, dressed in sweats and bare-chested. He was dripping with perspiration, a fierce frown on his face, hair damp. The scar on his back was a jagged line and Nessa's heart squeezed.

He gave the bag a thump so hard that Nessa felt the reverberations go through her own body. And then he stopped suddenly. She realised that he'd seen her in the mirror.

He turned around, chest heaving and gleaming.

Nessa was breathless. She'd never seen him looking so raw. Unconstructed. Suddenly the thought of never being with this man again left her breathless with pain. She couldn't do it. Even if he didn't really love her.

He stood with an arrested expression on his face and she walked towards him slowly. As she came closer the expression was replaced with a smooth mask. He pulled off his gloves and picked up a towel, running it roughly over his face and the back of his neck. He pulled on a T-shirt.

'I thought you were in Merkazad.'

Nessa stopped a few feet away. 'I was. I came back.' *Brilliant, Nessa. As if that weren't patently obvious.*

He shook his head. 'Why did you go there? You'd just lost our baby, but you jumped to your sister's bidding with no thought of the pain it might cause you?'

Our baby. Not *it*. Nessa's heart clenched. 'It wasn't like that. Iseult didn't know about the baby, and I thought it would be a good idea to help out.'

'You were afraid I'd propose again.' Luc sounded grim.

Nessa nodded slowly. 'Part of me was afraid you'd insist...' And that she wouldn't be able to say no.

'Was my proposal so unwelcome?' There was a bleak tone to his voice now.

Nessa nodded, watching his expression carefully. Something flashed in his eyes and she recognised pain. As much as she hated to see it, it also sent hope to her heart.

She moved closer and saw a wary look cross his face now.

'But not because of why you think. I couldn't bear the fact that it was such a clinical proposal. To merge two names. To bolster your reputation and success. And just because you'd had a revelation about wanting a family.'

He shook his head and when he spoke his voice was rough. 'It wasn't just that.'

He looked at her, and the pain in the depths of his eyes was unmistakable now. 'I'm sorry for everything. You just tried to help your brother and I treated you as if you'd stolen from me yourself. Then I seduced you, when I had no right to take your innocence, an innocence that I didn't believe in until it was too late. I had no right to disrupt your life like that.'

He went pale. 'When I saw you lying under those horses, I thought I'd killed you…and then the baby. It's my fault you lost the baby, Nessa. If I hadn't asked you to ride in the race it wouldn't have happened. You were innocent of every charge I levelled at you.'

Suddenly Nessa felt cold. She put a hand to her mouth, horror coursing through her. 'You feel responsible? That's why you were so upset when you saw the accident. I thought…'

Nessa felt sick and turned away before he could see her. She'd never felt like such a fool. She tried to walk away as quickly as she could but a hand on her arm stopped her.

'You thought what…?'

Nessa blinked back tears and turned around, avoiding Luc's eye. 'I watched the race online. You ran over, and you shouted at Francois that you cared about me, and not the horse.' But now Nessa realised that of course Luc would care about any one of his jockeys more than a horse.

That was all it had been.

His hand tightened so much on her arm that she looked up at him. When she saw the look on his face she stopped breathing.

'You thought I just felt responsible for you?'

Nessa's humiliation turned to anger. 'Didn't you?'

His eyes were burning and she saw the same volatile emotion she was feeling reflected in their depths. But she didn't trust it.

'Believe me,' he said grimly, 'I wish that what I felt for you was just a sense of responsibility.'

'What's that supposed to mean?'

He dropped his hand from her arm as if suddenly aware he might be hurting her.

'I proposed to you in the hospital because I was too cowardly to admit that I nearly lost my whole life when I saw you lying under that horse. Of course I felt responsible, but I was also terrified.'

He took a deep breath. 'I was terrified I was about to lose the only other person I've ever truly loved in my life, but I couldn't admit that to myself even then.'

Nessa's heart stopped. She was afraid she might be projecting words from her heart onto Luc's lips. 'What are you saying?'

He took a step closer. He looked uncharacteristically vulnerable. 'I'm saying that I love you, Nessa. I think I've loved you from the moment we met, when I knew that I didn't want to let you out of my sight. But I know you don't love me and I told myself I wouldn't stoop low enough to seduce you again because you deserve more. I brought nothing but more loss into your life.'

Nessa shook her head, almost too afraid to move in case she shattered this delicate moment. 'First of all, it's no one's fault we lost the baby. It was just one of those things. Secondly, I lied to you. I *do* love you. So much that it scares me. And third of all, you brought nothing but richness into my life. You awakened me. You made me believe I was beautiful, you gave me the chance to be a jockey, you showed me Paris. That's where I knew I loved you.'

He reached for her and drew her to him as gently as if she were spun glass. 'Do you mean this?'

She nodded. 'I mean it with every bone in my body. When I told you I didn't love you at the hospital it was because I thought you were just consolidating your empire with a marriage of convenience.'

He shook his head, drawing her in even closer so their bodies were touching. A wave of need surged through Nessa. Luc's voice was full of self-recrimination. 'None of this means anything without you. I said it wasn't about love because I didn't know what love was. Until I went back the next day and you were gone. I was so sure I could persuade you...seduce you. And then I realised I wanted so much more.

'I want it all, Nessa. A real family. Even though it terrifies me. How do I know how to have a family when I've never been part of one?'

Nessa reached up and put her arms around Luc's neck. She felt stupidly shy all of a sudden. 'I can show you.'

He looked down at her, a suspiciously bright glint in his eye. 'It might take a lifetime.'

'I wouldn't settle for anything less.'

Luc suddenly looked serious. He framed her face with his hands. 'Nessa O'Sullivan, I'm never letting you out of my sight, ever again. Will you marry me?'

She nodded, a surge of joy spreading from her heart to every part of her body. Tears made her vision blurry. 'Yes...yes, I will. I love you, Luc.'

'I love *you, mon amour.*'

Luc could feel Nessa's heart thumping in time with his, and as her mouth opened under his and he pulled her even closer he knew that this wasn't just a mirage, and that, finally, he'd found peace, love, and his true home.

EPILOGUE

'AND IT'S NESSA BARBIER, riding to glory again in the Kilkenny Stakes on Sacre Coeur, owned by her husband and brother-in-law...'

A short time later Luc watched as his wife rode into the winner's enclosure, mud-spattered face beaming. She wore the colours of the newly announced Barbier-Al-Saqr racing consortium—green and gold, a nod to Ireland and Merkazad.

His heart-rate finally returned to normal to see her in one piece. She saw him and her smile got even wider. She jumped off the horse gracefully and handed it to a groom before coming over to where he was standing with their two-year-old son, Cal, in his arms.

Flashes of light went berserk around them—the press still couldn't get enough of Luc and Nessa ever since their fairy-tale romance had become news. They'd been married almost two years ago in a modest ceremony in an old chapel on Luc's stud farm grounds in Kildare, and then they'd celebrated with a more lavish reception in Merkazad.

'You do know that every time I watch you race it takes about a year off my life?' Luc grumbled good-naturedly as he handed over his son, who was reaching for his mother with chubby arms.

Nessa cuddled him close and looked up at Luc. She had an enigmatic glint in her eye and then said *sotto voce*, 'Well, if it's any consolation it looks like this will be my last race for about a year, if not longer.'

Luc looked at her. The only other time she'd stopped racing was when they'd fallen pregnant with Cal, and even though the doctor had assured them that Nessa should be fine to race early in her pregnancy they'd both agreed that she wouldn't, in deference to what had happened when she'd first been pregnant.

A surge of emotion rushed through Luc as he reached for her. 'You're…?' He stopped, mindful of waggling ears.

She nodded, eyes shimmering with emotion. 'I'm late, so I don't know for sure yet, but I'm pretty certain.'

Luc pulled her and Cal into him, her free arm wrapped around his waist and his son snuggled up between them. His heart was so full he was afraid it might explode. He finally knew the true meaning of wealth and success and it had nothing to do with professional respect or money. It was *this*.

And then over Nessa's head he saw Nadim and Iseult with their two children walking towards them. Iseult was pregnant again with baby number three.

His family. Luc finally felt like he belonged to something he'd never had the courage to hope for, and it still felled him sometimes. How lucky he was. How blessed he was. And now this, the seed of a new life in Nessa's belly.

Nessa looked up at him and for a brief moment before they were enveloped in their family, and congratulations, they shared a look of pure love and understanding. 'I love you,' he said, not caring about hiding his emotion.

'I love you too…'

The kiss they shared at that moment with their son between them was the picture used on the front pages of the newspapers the next day under the headline: *Love at the races…a true family affair.*

* * * * *

If you enjoyed
THE VIRGIN'S DEBT TO PAY
you're sure to enjoy these other stories
by Abby Green!

A DIAMOND FOR THE SHEIKH'S MISTRESS
A CHRISTMAS BRIDE FOR THE KING
CLAIMED FOR THE DE CARRILLO TWINS
MARRIED FOR THE TYCOON'S EMPIRE

Available now!

Available May 22, 2018

#3625 DA ROCHA'S CONVENIENT HEIR
Vows for Billionaires
by Lynne Graham

Zac's convenient wedding to Freddie will provide him with an heir.
He's confident their passion will burn out, but when Freddie falls
pregnant, Zac realizes he craves more than just his legacy!

#3626 THE TYCOON'S SCANDALOUS PROPOSITION
Marrying a Tycoon
by Miranda Lee

Actress Kate is used to the spotlight, but nothing compares to
billionaire Blake's scorching gaze or their sizzling night together!
But when he offers her a starring role in his bed—dare she say
yes?

#3627 BILLIONAIRE'S BRIDE FOR REVENGE
Rings of Vengeance
by Michelle Smart

Benjamin's plan for vengeance is to steal and marry his enemy's
fiancée, Freya! It's meant to be a convenient arrangement. Yet
there's nothing remotely convenient about the red-hot pleasures
of their wedding night...

#3628 KIDNAPPED FOR HIS ROYAL DUTY
Stolen Brides
by Jane Porter

Desert prince Dal must find a replacement for his stolen bride
immediately. So he kidnaps his shy secretary, and expertly
seduces her! Will Poppy be persuaded to accept his royal
proposal?

#3629 BLACKMAILED BY THE GREEK'S VOWS
Conveniently Wed!
by Tara Pammi
Discovering her passionate marriage was a business deal devastated Valentina. Yet before granting a divorce, Kairos demands she play his wife again. And soon their intense fire is reignited...

#3630 A DIAMOND DEAL WITH HER BOSS
by Cathy Williams
While pretending to be her sexy boss Gabriel's fiancée, Abby can't resist the temptation of a burning-hot affair. But soon Abby must decide: Can she share her body—*and* soul—with Gabriel?

#3631 THE SHEIKH'S SHOCK CHILD
One Night With Consequences
by Susan Stephens
When innocent laundress Millie succumbs to Sheikh Khalid's touch, she's overwhelmed by the intensity of their encounter. But becoming Khalid's mistress isn't the only consequence of their reckless desire...and Millie's scandalous news will bind them permanently!

#3632 CLAIMING HIS PREGNANT INNOCENT
by Maggie Cox
Lily doesn't expect her landlord to be gorgeous billionaire Bastian. Antagonism leads to a sensual encounter, and shocking consequences! They'll meet at the altar, but will a ring truly make Lily his?

Get 2 Free Books,

Plus 2 Free Gifts—

just for trying the Reader Service!

*When desert prince Dal's convenient bride is stolen,
he must find a replacement—immediately. Suddenly,
his shy secretary, Poppy, has been whisked away to
Dal's kingdom, Jolie…where she'll find herself tempted
by his expert seduction!*

Read on for a sneak preview of
Jane Porter*'s next story*
KIDNAPPED FOR HIS ROYAL DUTY,
part of the **STOLEN BRIDES** *miniseries.*

Before they came to Jolie, Dal would have described
Poppy as pretty, in a fresh, wholesome, no-nonsense sort
of way with her thick, shoulder-length brown hair, large
brown eyes and serious little chin.

But as Poppy entered the dining room, with its glossy
white ceiling and dark purple walls, she looked anything
but wholesome and no-nonsense.

She was wearing a silk gown the color of cherries,
delicately embroidered with silver threads, and instead
of her usual ponytail or chignon, her dark hair was down,
and long, elegant chandelier earrings dangled from her
ears. As she walked, the semisheer kaftan molded to her
curves.

"It seems I've been keeping you waiting," she said,
her voice pitched lower than usual and slightly breathless.
"Izba insisted on all this," she added, gesturing up toward
her face.

At first Dal thought she was referring to the ornate silver earrings that were catching and reflecting the light, but once she was seated across from him, he realized her eyes had been rimmed with kohl and her lips had been outlined and filled in with a soft plum-pink gloss. "You're wearing makeup."

"Quite a lot of it, too." She grimaced. "I tried to explain to Izba that this wasn't me, but she's very determined once she makes her mind up about something and apparently, dinner with you requires me to look like a tart."

Dal checked his smile. "You don't look like a tart. Unless it's the kind of tart one wants to eat."

Color flooded Poppy's cheeks and she glanced away, suddenly shy, and he didn't know if it was her shyness or the shimmering dress that clung to her, but he didn't think any woman could be more beautiful or desirable than Poppy right now. "You look lovely," he said quietly. "But I don't want you uncomfortable all through dinner. If you'd rather go remove the makeup, I'm happy to wait."

She looked at him closely, as if doubting his sincerity. "It's fun to dress up, but I'm worried Izba has the wrong idea about me."

"And what is that?"

"She seems to think you're going to…marry…me."

Don't miss
KIDNAPPED FOR HIS ROYAL DUTY
available June 2018.

And look for the second part of the **STOLEN BRIDES** *duet,*
THE BRIDE'S BABY OF SHAME by Caitlin Crews,
available July 2018 wherever
Harlequin Presents® books and ebooks are sold.

www.Harlequin.com